Additional

"An utter—and often h[ilarious?]... of mixing levity with t[...] ensure the narrative never becomes too heavy. Amid the investigative antics and hustle of daily life, familial love emerges as the linchpin of the story, echoing Uncle Will's unwavering belief that 'family is wondrous,' in spite of its imperfections."

—ALA *Booklist* (**starred review**)

"[A] cunning mystery by Tubb, in which a grieving tween's often laugh-aloud misadventures in detective work bring her estranged family closer together. Typical genre tropes are subverted in delightful ways; rather than solve this harrowing mystery alone, Chloe leans on her family (and Charlie), who tirelessly support her sleuthing antics."

—*Publishers Weekly* (**starred review**)

"Will delight kids and adults alike. A mystery unfolds within a compelling, joyful story of honoring a loved one by living in the moment."

—*Kirkus Reviews*

"A wonderfully told, thoughtful, and highly entertaining story of a busy family whose priorities have just been radically altered, and the story of a girl whose middle school life seems to be coming undone. Chloe needs to figure out what it really means to achieve Uncle Will's number one goal: 'Seize the day!'"

—Tim McCarthy, Boswell Book Company, Milwaukee, WI

"A charming, heartfelt, and funny middle grade mystery. I adored this book about family and grief and seizing the day!"

—Jen Steele, Boswell Book Company, Milwaukee, WI

Also by Kristin O'Donnell Tubb
A Dog Like Daisy
Zeus, Dog of Chaos
Luna Howls at the Moon
The Decompostion of Jack

FOWL PLAY

KRISTIN O'DONNELL TUBB

HarperCollins Children's Books,
a division of HarperCollins Publishers,
195 Broadway, New York, NY 10007

HarperCollins Publishers, Macken House,
39/40 Mayor Street Upper, Dublin 1, D01 C9W8, Ireland

Fowl Play
Copyright © 2024 by Kristin O'Donnell Tubb
All rights reserved. Manufactured in Robbinsville, NJ,
United States of America.
No part of this book may be used or reproduced in any manner whatsoever without written permission except in the case of brief quotations embodied in critical articles and reviews. Without limiting the exclusive rights of any author, contributor, or the publisher of this publication, any unauthorized use of this publication to train generative artificial intelligence (AI) technologies is expressly prohibited. HarperCollins also exercises their rights under Article 4(3) of the Digital Single Market Directive 2019/790 and expressly reserves this publication from the text and data mining exception.
harpercollins.com

Library of Congress Control Number: 2023940812
ISBN 978-0-06-327404-4

Typography by Molly Fehr
25 26 27 28 29 PC/CWR 10 9 8 7 6 5 4 3 2 1

First paperback edition, 2025

For Chloe, my fellow family artist

I

CARPE DIEM

When someone is good at shuffling a deck of cards, it's like a bird in flight—the smooth arch of the cards like wings, the tiny flutter of the deck like wingbeats. Tidy and perfect. My uncle Will could shuffle like that. He could look you in the eye, tell a joke, laugh, and slide the right number of cards across the table, tucked under your nested hands. Sometimes in my memories I still see him doing it. Anyway, when someone dies and they leave a last will and testament, that's what happens: their stuff gets shuffled up and dealt to the people sitting around the table, just like a deck of cards.

Whenever they read someone's last will and testament in the movies, it's in this big, dramatic office full of wood and leather, and all the tearstained folks clutch their pearls and wring their fur coats and blow their noses into silk hankies. Millions of dollars are doled out. Inheritances are claimed. Estates are settled, whatever that means.

Lies! Intrigue! Accusations of foul play!

But here I am, at my very first will reading, and I'm sitting in a too-hot car, staring at a dirty glass door in a strip mall. The door has *Cheatham Law Offices* painted on it. The office is sandwiched between a Subway and a store that sells aquariums and fish food, but no fish, apparently.

Mom fiddles with the air-conditioning, but it's still spewing hot air only. She huffs loudly. "AC needs to be fixed." She lifts her chin at the door in front of us before resting it on the steering wheel. "'Cheatham Law'—is this some kind of joke?"

Grammy licks her teeth. "I'm sure he's one of the most brilliant legal minds in all of Charleston."

"I'm sure," Mom says, shaking her head.

Jacob drums on Mom's headrest from the back seat. "This is awesome! A will reading! Uncle Will's will! Maybe he was a secret millionaire or something. Like maybe he won the lotto and didn't tell anyone? I bet he's leaving me a Lamborghini!"

Grammy is applying her vampire-red lipstick in the small sun-shield mirror. She raises an eyebrow at me in the mirror. I'm in the back seat behind her, so there's no mistaking Grammy's eyebrow sarcasm. She turns to Mom. "Well now, that's a possibility, isn't it, Teresa?"

Mom pinches her lips together. If I'd asked that question, she would've replied, *Don't be ridiculous. Will would never be able to keep a secret like that.* But since it's her mom asking it, she just pinches her lips, rolls her eyes.

I want to chuckle, but I don't. I've missed this—the four of us together, cutting up. Lately we're rarely in the same house at the same time. All of us in one car? Hasn't happened since . . . well, I can't remember when. We just need Uncle Will and Uncle Frank to make it truly complete. *A full house*, Uncle Will would say with a devilish grin, sliding all the poker chips into his pile on game night.

Mom cuts the engine of our Toyota Prius. The car keeps grumbling, sputters, coughs. She shakes her head and mutters, "This is all one last big gotcha, isn't it, Willie? A last act."

I smile to myself. It *is* something Uncle Will would do.

Mom slams open the car door—yes, open (really, my mom can slam just about anything, anywhere)—and strides toward Cheatham Law.

We all follow. Hey, maybe I'll get a yacht.

• • •

"Come in, come in!" A balding man, who I'm guessing is Mr. Cheatham, leaps up from his desk. His chair rolls backward and crashes into a dented green metal filing cabinet. He dashes around the desk and swipes a bunch of fast-food wrappers off two frayed chairs into an already-full garbage can.

Grammy licks her teeth—her "tell" for when she's displeased. Uncle Will taught me that. Both what a "tell" is, and that Grammy's tell is licking her teeth. She perches on the edge of one chair, her purse in her lap. Mom collapses into the other, but quickly scrambles to standing.

"It's wet!" she says.

Mr. Cheatham's eyes widen. "Here, let me get you—"

Mom sighs one of those mom sighs, the ones only moms can do. "I'll stand."

Uncle Frank wanders in and bends to hug Grammy. "What's this all about?" he whispers to Mom while kissing her cheek. "I can't imagine that Will had a will. I thought he sunk all his money into that mushroom farm."

Mom doesn't want to smile, but she does. "That made more sense than the alpacas."

Uncle Frank fist-bumps me and looks at me with pity-filled eyes. Ugh. It's the way everyone in my family has looked at me for the past three weeks.

"How're you doing, kiddo?" he says. Gives my shoulder a squeeze.

I smile too big and answer too loud. "Good! Got a goal in yesterday's match!" My fake enthusiasm is enough for now, I guess, because he nods and turns to Jacob.

"How's the Camaro running?"

"Loud and fast," Jacob says with a grin.

Mom grits her teeth. "Jake . . ."

Uncle Frank winks at Jacob and squeezes his biceps. "Bench pressing, what? One-forty now?"

"Ounces, maybe," I mutter. Uncle Frank and Jacob both hear me. Uncle Frank chuckles. Jacob frog-punches my upper arm.

"Oww-uh!" I say, rubbing my arm, exaggerating how much the punch hurt. "Mom!"

Uncle Frank puts Jacob in a gentle headlock. "Be nice to your sister, Jake," he says, and winks at Mom. "Sisters are here to bail you out of all your messes."

Mom's lips tighten. "That's not why we're here at all." But I can tell she's smiling underneath her pretend scowl.

Jacob and Uncle Frank have this special bond over football. They're a pair, those two. Watching them lightly punch each other makes my eyes blur. The uncle

I was closest to is now gone. There's no one here to make fun of these two goofballs with me.

Mom has Grammy. Jacob has Uncle Frank. And I have a stomachache.

Mr. Cheatham has unfolded squeaky metal chairs for the three of us. He disappears into a closet and wheels out a rusty cart. It has a TV on it. A weird clunky box is attached to the TV by several tangled wires.

"A VCR," Uncle Frank says. He raises an eyebrow at Grammy. They both got that cool eyebrow-raising gene. I'm bummed I didn't get it. "High-tech."

Jacob shrugs at me. We've both heard of a VCR, sure, but we've never seen one. Pretty unimpressive.

Mr. Cheatham clears his throat. He had chili for lunch. I can tell because his short-sleeved dress shirt is stained with it, and he smells like it. "Folks, welcome to the reading of Will Calhoun's last will and testament." He crams a clunky plastic box into the other clunky plastic box, and the TV flickers to life.

Uncle Will!

He's in his bright, sunny apartment, and he's wearing a Hawaiian shirt, a pirate's hat, and an eye patch. Tears sting my eyes. He looks so healthy. I'd forgotten how full his face used to look, how pink his cheeks were.

Mr. Cheatham pushes play.

"Family!" Uncle Will booms. The tears push themselves out of my eyes and take a stroll down my cheeks. Grammy is blinking a lot, and she has a wistful look on her face. Jacob beams at his on-screen uncle. Mom and Uncle Frank are stoic, Mom nibbling her lip. Uncle Will's memorial service was three long weeks ago.

And then came this. This will reading. It was *unexpected*.

Uncle Will likes to keep things that way. *Unexpected*.

It's weird to smile with tears on your cheeks.

"I'm so glad you came to the reading of my—ahem!—last will and testament." On-screen, Uncle Will pretends to straighten a tie he's not wearing. "If you're watching this, it's probably because I've died a horrific, mysterious death, and I need you to avenge my demise." Uncle Will widens his eyes at the camera, pauses. A long time. We all look around the room at each other. *What?!*

My mind spins: something *did* feel off about Uncle Will's death. We were told he was sick, but he kept us in the dark for so long . . . we all wondered what *exactly* had happened.

Uncle Will bursts into deep laughter. "Kidding! I kid! Listen, I know most folks don't do this sort of thing anymore, gather around after someone's died to hear how his stuff gets divvied up. But my lawyer there with you—Mark Cheatham? Mark, take a bow!"

Uncle Will pauses at this point, waiting for Mr. Cheatham to bow before us in the here and now. Instead, Mr. Cheatham blushes and gives us a small wave.

Uncle Will continues: "Mark lost to me bad in a poker game last year. I mean, BAD. Right, Mark?" He chuckles on-screen.

Mr. Cheatham burns crimson and nods at his stained carpet.

Uncle Will shines through the old TV. "But Mark was broke. 'Mark,' I said, 'I got us a way you can pay me back.' And so Mark, being the good buddy that he is, agreed to draw up my last will and testament. And not just draw it up! He agreed to call an old-timey will-and-testament reading! So congratulations, folks! You are gathered here today because Mark Cheatham lost at poker and couldn't pay."

I expect to see Mr. Cheatham blushing practically purple at this point, but instead, his eyes are glassy, and he chuckles.

He was a good friend to my uncle. That's clear. My tears start again.

"So listen. I know Teresa is out there champing at

the bit to get started." We all look at Mom, who immediately stops biting her lip and purses them instead.

"I'm going to start with my baby brother, Frank." Uncle Frank sits up straight in the metal folding chair. It groans. He looks pained, like he's about to be on the receiving end of a headlock from his older brother.

"Frank. I leave you my vast collection of Robin Hood paraphernalia. Do NOT sell it on eBay—you will NOT get what it's worth." Uncle Will lifts his eye patch and gives his brother a stern look out of the TV. Mr. Cheatham has disappeared into the closet again, and when he emerges, he plunks a cardboard box on Uncle Frank's lap.

"Robin Hood collection?" Uncle Frank asks. He lifts and studies the item on top—a green felt hat pierced with a red feather.

"There's some other stuff in there, too, brother. Valuable stuff. All my marked-up Agatha Christie novels. My kazoo collection. My second-place Frisbee golf trophy. I trust you'll know what to do with it."

Uncle Frank digs out a worn copy of *And Then There Were None*, with dog-eared pages and sticky notes jutting out in all directions. He shifts his jaw and sighs.

"Cool!" Jacob says, bouncing on his chair. Uncle Frank narrows his eyes at the screen.

"Teresa and Mom," Uncle Will says. He's just as charming in this video as he was in real life. "I leave you my photo albums. They are . . . priceless." Uncle Will gets a bit choked up there. I've never seen his photo albums, but it makes perfect sense to me that he'd consider them his most priceless items. Uncle Will was all about carpe diem and taking selfies of us, even when we were just doing stupid stuff like building Legos.

Mr. Cheatham hands five or six photo albums to Grammy. She hugs them tightly to her chest, and the plastic inside them crinkles. It's the perfect gift for her. And it makes Mom happy to see her mom happy.

Uncle Will always knew how to do that. Start a happiness domino chain.

"Jacob, my man!" Uncle Will shouts through the tinny TV speakers.

"I'm here for you, bro!" Jacob shouts back at the screen. I roll my eyes but grin.

Uncle Will holds up a square piece of cardboard on-screen. "I hereby bequeath to you: my album collection!"

Mr. Cheatham hefts two milk crates, each filled with record albums. Like, vinyl records. He plunks the crates next to Jacob. Dust motes fly everywhere.

On-screen, Uncle Will slides a record out of its

sleeve and holds it up to the camera. Light bounces off the black plastic surface.

"Music sounds best on vinyl," Uncle Will whispers, staring at the album like it's a thing of beauty. He runs a fingertip over the album's surface. "LPs are the best. Trust me on this, Jaybird."

Jacob imitates Uncle Will, sliding a black album out of its sleeve and gazing at it lovingly. "Yeah . . ." He nods with deep seriousness. "Vinyl."

Mom looks at Uncle Frank and whispers, "Of course we don't have a turntable."

Uncle Will composes himself and looks at the camera. I swear it feels like he's looking at *me*. "And finally, Chloe. Chlo-dog. My favorite niece." I am his only niece, but that always makes me smile, every time he says it.

Said it.

Whew. More tears.

"I'm leaving you the thing that means the most to my heart. Mi compadre. My partner in crime. My best friend. I'm leaving you . . ."

He dashes off-screen, then hops back into the picture with a—

Is that a—

"My parrot, Charlie!" Uncle Will shouts. The gray bird on his shoulder flusters. The pirate getup makes sense now.

Mom squints at the screen in disbelief. "A *bird*, Will?!" she shouts at the TV.

"Best friend?" Uncle Frank blinks. "When did he get a bird?"

Mr. Cheatham emerges from his magic closet with, yep, a bird.

"Pretty bird! Pretty bird!" the bird squawks. He makes a loud clicking sound—*click-click!*—and flaps his massive wings, like he's trying to make his way over to me. In a daze, I hold up my forearm.

The bird whistles and hops right onto the sleeve of my hoodie. He's large—as tall as a stack of seven or eight books—so it surprises me when he's light, weighing about the same as a can full of Coke. And he's beautiful. Silvery gray, with feather tips like glitter. And his tail is brilliant, beautiful red—so bright it looks like his tail feathers were dipped in red paint.

Uncle Will is stroking this same bird on TV. "Chloe, meet Charles Featherington the Second. Charlie, for short. Named for King Charles the Second, of course." King Charles II—our city, Charleston, South Carolina, was also named for him.

"Hi, Charlie," I whisper. I reach a finger forward and stroke the feathers on top of his head. They're as soft and light as dandelion fluff. Charlie closes his eyes and nuzzles my hand. He coos lightly. My heart coos, too.

"A *bird*?!" Mom repeats.

"A bird!" Uncle Frank says. He leaps to his feet and kicks the box holding the Robin Hood knickknacks. "A *bird* is your best friend, Will? Seriously?" Uncle Frank kicks the box again and again, muttering things like *so selfish* and *just awful* and *terrible brother*. Mom lays a gentle hand on Frank's shoulder, and he stops, wild-eyed and panting. The box is crumpled and dented. Robin Hood paraphernalia is everywhere.

Uncle Frank storms out of the office, leaving the box behind. He tries to slam the front door behind him, but it's one of those heavy swinging doors, so he ends up just pulling it shut frantically in a tantrum.

Grammy's eyes are closed and she's doing her yogic breathing. Mom paces.

"Maybe I'll go make sure he's okay," Jacob says. He stands, cracks his knuckles.

Grammy shakes her head. "He's fine. Just needs more time, is all."

Jacob nods. For some reason, that wads my emotions up into a tight paper ball. *He needs more time.* Why didn't Uncle Will get more time?

"Pretty bird. Pretty bird," Charlie says, and chirps.

"Cool!" Jacob says.

"Cool!" Charlie repeats. "Cool! Cool!" He whistles.

"Cool," I say. I suddenly can't stop smiling. "Thank you, Uncle Will." I don't say more, but I feel it: *He's perfect. Just like you were. Thank you.*

But Uncle Will doesn't hear me. He's on TV with TV-Charlie, dancing to the Beatles. *Blackbird singing in the dead of night . . .*

Until he stops.

He looks right at the camera. Right at me.

"I love you, family. Family is wondrous. That's all you need to know. Family is wondrous. Make it all count, okay? *Make every moment together count. Carpe diem!*"

My heart leaps into my throat. All the tension that has been hanging over me since the beginning of this, all the questions and anger and hostility about Uncle Will's illness, looming over my head like a storm cloud—none of that is here in this sunny, music-filled video. I don't know what to do with that. Can you just shove all that anger aside?

"I will, Uncle Will," I whisper. "I promise." I look around at my family. Jacob, drumming on the chair next to him, impatient to leave and check on Uncle Frank. Grammy, clutching Uncle Will's photos, impatient with mourning and grief. Mom, pacing and eyeing Charlie, impatient to mutter bad things about this bird the whole way home.

Impatient to move and push past and *go go go*. Maybe that's what carpe diem is—cramming as much as you possibly can into a day. Isn't that how you make every moment count?

My family is all pacing feet and clenched fists and tight jaws. I alter my promise: "I'll try my best, Uncle Will."

2

EMERGENCY DANCE PARTY!

Charles Featherington the Second. Charlie. She's a she, I find out once I get home and flip through the book that came with her. *Your African Grey Parrot and You.* Charlie nibbles at the pages as I read, and bits of paper fall around us like confetti. This book has been nibbled a lot. Little nips dot every page.

I also find a bill from a veterinarian noting that Charlie's wings are clipped. I flinch; I hope it didn't hurt her. According to the book, that means that Charlie can't really fly. She can sail down from high places, but to get up, she has to climb, hop, or be placed there. She can go down but not up. These days, I can relate.

Finally, there's a small harness with a leash, just like for a tiny dog. I gently fold each of Charlie's wings under the loops and snap the harness closed. I clip the length of the leash to the tiny silver loop on her back and string the other end over my wrist. How about that! Walking a bird!

"Cheerio!" Charlie squawks. "Cheerio, mate! Long live the Queen!"

I laugh. Charlie copies Uncle Will's imitation of a British accent, which is actually a horrible mishmash of Scottish, Australian, and Irish, all tinged with the Southern drawl of Charleston. It's like having Uncle Will nearby, hearing her awful accent. My heart warms, and my memory flashes to Uncle Will bowing deeply, presenting my mom with a fistful of scraggly daisies. *M'lady*, he said, to which my mom replied, *Stop it, Will. We're going to be late.*

I get these memory flashes of Uncle Will all the time now. Grammy calls old photos "snapshots." That's what these thoughts of Will are like: memory snapshots. I can feel them; they sting. *Snap! Shot!*

Our cat, Friendly (who is anything but), sniffs the air from under the coffee table. Her ears are pasted back, and her whiskers twitch. "No way, Friendly," I say. "Charlie is not lunch." I reach out to touch the cat, and she leaps in surprise, banging her head on the underside of the table. Charlie squawks and flaps her wings, feathers flying. Friendly growls and scampers from the room, tail as puffy as a toilet brush.

Their first meeting went well.

Charlie nips at her feathers and pulls out a beakful of them. She spits them on the bottom of her small travel cage. I notice she's got a few bald patches here and there, so I look it up. *Your African Grey Parrot and You* says this kind of overpreening might be due to stress or big changes. "Ditto, birdie," I whisper to her, and run a finger down her soft back. She blinks.

"Cowabunga! Shrimp on the barbie!" Charlie clicks twice and cocks her head at me as she says this, like it's code for something. The feathers on top of her head ruffle like a mohawk. She whistles.

Shrimp? Maybe she's hungry?

"Here you go," I say, and dump some crunchy bits that look like granola into a small Tupperware dish. She pecks at it, picks it up with one of her gray, clawed legs, and hurls it across our living room. I laugh. Mom sees this from the kitchen and sighs so heavily, I'm surprised I don't feel a gust of wind.

I perch Charlie on my shoulder. She whistles her approval. I find Jacob in his bedroom. He's flexing his wee muscles in front of his full-length mirror, but I don't make fun because I need his help.

"Help me set up Charlie's birdcage," I say to his flexed reflection.

Jacob tries to make his pecs dance, but it looks more like he's shrugging alternate shoulders. "Can't, Squeak.

Football practice." He drops his shoulders, grabs his keys, and pushes past me out the door.

I hate it when he calls me Squeak. Short for "Pip-squeak." I'm almost as tall as him now.

I find Grammy locked in the hallway bathroom. "Grammy. Let's teach Charlie some new words."

Grammy is sneaking a cigarette behind the locked door. I can smell it. I'd never rat her out to Mom, but *gah*, it stinks.

"Can't, darling," Grammy breathes through the door. "I'm getting ready to head to bridge at the senior center. I'm going to beat that Mildred Hastings today if I have to wrestle her to the ground and yank those cards right out of her hands, the dirty cheater."

I grin. She'd do it, too. No one messes with my grammy. She is old-school Charleston. Born and raised here, which means she's as salty as our city. I go back into the living room and peek into the kitchen. Friendly has slinked in and is weaving around Mom's ankles, obviously lobbying to be the best pet. "Mom, want to help me with—"

"Absolutely not," she says, eyeing Charlie on my shoulder. "Look at those claws! And that beak! That bird is terrifying." Mom shudders. Charlie plucks out a feather and spits it at her. Friendly hisses. I giggle.

Mom swipes up her phone and types. She must be making her to-do list, because she mutters, "Haircut.

Grammy's dentist appointment. Get the car fixed . . ." She looks up at me like I was helping her list all that stuff. "Target run. Need anything?"

"Help with this bird," I mumble. I head back to the living room, where we're planning to set up Charlie's massive birdcage. I wanted Charlie in my room with me, but my room's not big enough for this contraption. This cage is as big as a golf cart. Mr. Cheatham brought it over from Will's apartment, disassembled, in his rusty old pickup.

I sigh and plop on the couch. "No one around again today, bird." Doors slam and cars start, and they all go away.

"But I got you now, Charlie," I say.

She poops on our carpet and makes a sound like she's blowing a raspberry, *bbblllppphhtt*.

I thought putting together a massive birdcage would be like putting together a Lego kit—follow the directions, get the thing pictured on the front of the box.

But there are tools involved. Screwdrivers and screws and tiny plastic bits. Those things are small and frustrating. I try breaking up my anger through a little chat with my new friend, Charlie.

"So, Charlie," I say, squinting at the dark, hard-to-reach corner of the cage where the next screw goes.

"Mr. Cheatham says Will got you just after Christmas. Won you in a poker game. That was right when Will . . ." I don't want to say it, not even to a bird, so I change the subject.

"Have you ever seen a busier family than this one? 'I gotta go here. I gotta be there.' Always in six thousand directions, always so serious about everything. Grades! Soccer! Vegetables! Ugh. I'm so sick of it."

Charlie says a word that sounds like "Skull! Skull!" I chuckle. Charlie's "words" are more like noises, punctuated with random clicks and whistles.

My screwdriver skids out of the screw slot, and I skin three knuckles. I need a break.

"Emergency dance party!" I hear Uncle Will shout in my head. Snapshot! I smile, whip out my phone, and pull up my Emergency Dance Party playlist. Bill Withers's "Lovely Day" sings out of my phone. Uncle Frank's favorite song. I wonder if he's still mad. Dude can hold a grudge. He once stayed mad at Uncle Will for two months after Will wouldn't stop prank calling him. *Is your refrigerator running?* So ridiculous and *so* funny. Even Mom laughed and told Frank to lighten up. Whew. Snapshot.

Charlie sits on top of a couch pillow, slowly plucking the stitching out of the seam with her beak and claws. I probably should've stopped her from doing that, but I couldn't watch her *and* put this cage together.

The minute the chorus of the song starts, Charlie freezes. Then she begins bobbing her head up and down, up and down. She sidles to the edge of the couch, then slides to the other end, a bit like moonwalking.

"Go, Charlie!" I shout. "Look at your dance moves!"

"Pretty girl! Go, Charlie!" she shouts back. *Click-click!* She whistles like she's singing along with the music.

Charlie bobs and weaves and hops across the back of the couch while I spin and leap and twirl across the living room floor.

"Emergency dance party!" Charlie shouts, and I laugh-cry—she sounds just like Uncle Will. I dash over and give her a small kiss on top of her head. She blows another raspberry, *bbblllppphhtt.*

Friendly watches all this from her perch on a bookshelf. Her tail twitches with supreme disapproval.

Charlie fluffs her feathers, I punch the air. When the song winds down, Charlie curls one of her wings over her head, ducks beneath it. She murmurs, "Where's Will?"

My shoulders drop—she misses him so much. "What? Are you looking for Will, Charlie?" But she's sleepy. She sighs softly.

I grin at her and snap a photo with my phone.

"Good night, Charlie," I say.

"Good night, Charlie," she says, muffled, from under her wing. "It was murder."

My heart lurches.

"What?" I ask. I rush to her side. "What did you say, Charlie?" But she's a bird. She's not going to just repeat herself.

I blink. I misheard her, I bet. Her little bird voice sounds like hearing a message through a set of walkie-talkies. Sometimes it's crystal clear, sometimes it's crackly. My heart calms.

I run a finger down her down her back, across her soft feathers.

"I'll learn your words soon," I promise her. "I'm sorry I don't understand everything yet. It's hard to be misunderstood."

As if on cue, my dad texts: **Soccer practice today, right? Focus on that footwork, kiddo!**

And then another snapshot memory of Uncle Will, throwing an arm over my shoulder after a big loss. *You win some, you lose some, Chlo-dog. I mean, look: you won the uncle lottery! How lucky can one person get?*

3

THE ONE THING I DON'T HAVE

I look at the clock on the microwave. "Oh, crap! I gotta knock out my art project before soccer practice." I hold my arm up to Charlie, and she hops on board. "Shotgun!" she cackles, like she's calling the passenger seat. I smile. It's fun having a sidekick who rides on your arm like this.

In my room, I spread a blank canvas and some oil paints across my desk. Brushes. A palette. A bottle of linseed oil. I perch Charlie on the footboard of my bed and offer her a paintbrush. She grabs it with her claw and twiddles it across her knuckles like a professional drummer. She holds the brushy fibers up to her beak and starts plucking the hairs out one by one.

I turn back to my supplies and sigh. I love art. I love collage. I love pottery. I love sketching. But I hate painting.

Check that—I love painting, too. Or rather, I love crinkly tubes of gem-colored oil paints. I love pots of watercolors, and the clouds the brushes make when you swish them through a cup of water. I love the nutty smell of linseed oil, and how it thins out dollops of shiny paint, makes it as smooth as lip gloss. I love tiny dollops of shiny paint, spread around a palette like a small, colorful army of snails. I love how the palette looks like a painting itself after a painting is done.

I hate a blank canvas. It's so . . . intimidating. The paint I eventually slosh across a white canvas never looks as stunning as the painting that lives in my head.

"Landscape," I mutter. It's our assignment, due tomorrow. Paint a landscape. I should've started it earlier. My art teacher, Ms. Umar, loves landscapes and especially loves painting them. She says, "Painting is just another way of keeping a diary." Then she tells us Pablo Picasso said that. And *then* she tells us Pablo Picasso was a bit of a creep, and that we should not google him. Which of course makes us all google him.

She's a great teacher. So cool. She wears these amazing bright clothes and headdresses from her home country, Nigeria, and her personality is that way, too—colorful and bold and bright. I really want her to love my art.

Ms. Umar is big on "paint what inspires you." I decide to paint from a photo I took of Asheville, North Carolina, last summer. It's where my dad lives, about four hours away from Charleston, and it's in the Blue Ridge Mountains—roll after roll of purple, blue, and green ridges. They look like waves on the ocean, with wisps of clouds kissing the peaks like cotton candy. The orange sunset behind the last hill tints the whole sky the color of apricots.

I inhale. I swipe on my first mountain. Purple.

No, too purply.

I thin it out with some blue.

Now it's too blue.

Grammy's back, and she jangles by on the way to her bedroom, her big jewelry clattering. She barely glances at the canvas and says, "Try purple." More purple? Hmmph.

"That's what I'm trying to correct!" I shout after her as she clanks down the hall.

Maybe it needs some green?

I hear the door downstairs open and close three or four times. Mom's back, too, moving in groceries, muttering about how she's lugged these bags for blocks because "the parking around here stinks." I look at my watch. I have to hurry.

I mix in some yellow. Ugh—no! Black? *Gah!* I smear and slosh and dot paint. I try to pull back—Ms. Umar is always telling us to *pull back*—but it's too late.

My purple mountains majesty look more like heaping brown piles of manure.

"Chloe, come on!" Mom shouts upstairs. "We're going to be late!"

I sigh and look at Charlie. She's plucked every last fiber out of the cheap paintbrush I gave her and is now tapping the wand against my bed frame like a drumstick. A ticking clock.

"Pretty bird," Charlie says. "Say please and thank you!"

"I'm trying to do what you said, Uncle Will," I whisper, looking at Charlie. "I'm trying to carpe diem. I'm trying to cram as much as I can into one day, but it doesn't seem to be working."

"Chloe, let's go!"

Painting takes the one thing I don't have: time.

Dad FaceTimes me that evening. "How was practice, kiddo?"

I shrug. "Okay. Still having some trouble with my left-footed pass."

He smiles and nods. "How do you get to Carnegie Hall?" It's an old musician's joke, apparently, and the answer is *practice, practice, practice*. He says it to me every time we talk about soccer, which is every day.

On my screen, I see Charlie behind me, strutting across the footboard of my bed.

"Hey! How's the bird?" Dad says with a grin.

My insides light up, fizzy and happy like I just took a swig of Coke. "Great! I mean, she's a lot of work, but great! Mom hates her."

Dad laughs. "I bet. Leave it to Will to do something like this."

He doesn't mean to be cruel, but it feels a bit like a playground shove. Like too much horseplay. He must've seen me flinch, because his face softens.

"How're you doing, kiddo?"

"I'm good," I lie. Well, it's not a *total* lie. I'm good, for the most part. But the other parts, the Will parts . . . Dad sees this, too.

"Losing somebody like Will—" Dad exhales through tight lips. "That's hard. Really the toughest part of living. Of loving. Have you talked to anyone about it? Mom or Grammy?"

I shake my head. It hurts too much. For all of us.

I don't say that part out loud, but he seems to see that, too. Some dads can see the things that aren't even said. It's both awesome and annoying.

"When your mom and I separated—" *Oh lawsy, here we go.* My dad loves to be *so open* about all this stuff. Total cringe. "—my therapist told me to keep a journal. Write it all down. She called it a word purge, like vomiting." He chuckles. "But you know? It helps. Maybe you should do that. Write down the things you want to remember about Will."

I grin. "He used to write down words he loved, remember? Had that beat-up notepad and he'd write down words he wanted to collect. Words like *harbinger* and *wistful*."

Dad chuckles. "I remember! Always called himself a word collector. That's the kind of thing I'm talking about, Bug. Write down those memories. Because here's the thing: You'll forget them if you don't. Even if you think you won't. And you really don't want to forget them."

He's right. It's only been a few weeks, and I'm already fuzzy on things like which was his favorite ball cap and if he drank sweet tea or plain.

Charlie ripples her feathers, lifts her wings, and *leaps!*

"Charlie!" I shout.

She flaps her wings frantically, but she can't lift. She tumbles to the floor, crumpling like a thrown sock.

"Charlie, are you okay?"

The camera on my end of the screen spins wildly. "Is she okay, Bug?" Dad asks. "Is Charlie all right?"

Charlie shakes like a wet dog, rearranging her wings, her feathers. She blinks, clicks twice, and cocks her head at me. "Ripper, mate!" she says with a bad Australian accent. "Pretty bird!" She whistles as I scoop her up, like she's saying thank you. *Your African Grey Parrot and You* says birds don't like to be on the ground; they instinctively know how light and fragile they are, and they feel vulnerable down there. Birds need height.

"She's okay," I say, and lift Charlie to the phone to show my dad.

"Whew!" Dad says through the camera. "I couldn't tell what happened. Charlie, you scared us!" He means it, too. Dad loves animals. He'd be totally okay with Charlie living there.

We say our goodbyes, Dad singsonging, "See you in a few weeks, kiddo! I'm so excited for you and Jake to visit."

It's quiet, and I stroke the feathers down Charlie's back. She closes her eyes.

"Homicide," she murmurs.

I blink. My heart skips a beat. "What, Charlie?" I whisper frantically. "What did you say?"

"Homicide de-trek-er. De-trek-tive! De-trek-tive!"

"Homicide detective?" I whisper again, but the bird is asleep.

My stomach churns. How could she possibly know a phrase like that?

4

GOLLY WHAT A DAY

Summer is almost here, so I open my windows at night to sleep. I love the sound of the low-country frogs and crickets singing. Tonight, their harmonies are accompanied by Mom and Grammy on the patio below, drinking an "adult beverage" (Grammy's words) and going through Uncle Will's "box of junk" (Mom's words). I lie on my bed, stare at the ceiling, and eavesdrop.

"I can't believe Frank, just leaving this stuff behind at that sham of a lawyer's office," Mom says. She rustles through the deep bin. "What is this?"

"It's a coffee mug, dear."

I can hear Mom smirking from here. "Not that. This. These words."

"It's that song they sing in the movie, Teresa," Grammy says. "You know. 'Oo-de-lally, golly what a day'? Have you forgotten your entire childhood?"

"Will sure hasn't," Mom mutters. She pauses. "I can't believe the *nerve* of him, leaving that bird to Chloe."

Grammy giggles. "It was brilliant. Will was always playing chess while the rest of us were playing checkers."

"Will was always playing *poker*," Mom says. She sucks in a sharp breath. "He knows I can't get rid of it now. It's her bird, not mine. He left it to her on purpose."

"Yep." Grammy takes a loud sip of something.

"I mean, if he'd left the bird to me, it would be long gone already. I would've found a bird rescue organization, or some weird old biddy who needed another member for her flock."

Mom is getting worked up now, and Grammy's giggling turns into full-on laughter.

"Mom, stop laughing at me," my mom says. "I'm serious! Those birds can live to be eighty! *Eighty!* That bird's going to outlive me!"

Grammy wheezes with laughter. "Probably."

Mom is chuckling now, too. She's still angry, but Grammy has unwound her anger. Loosened it like a rusty screw. I wish I knew how to do that. "This is just like Will, trying to get the last laugh," Mom says.

Grammy sighs through her heavy giggles. I imagine she's wiping a tear from the corner of her eye; she cries every time she laughs. More so now that Will is gone. "Well, it's working, then, isn't it?"

Mom huffs a laugh. "I guess." She rummages more. "Oh! His laptop is in here!"

"Hmmm," Grammy says, sipping again. She's not much for technology.

It sounds like Mom is studying the laptop. I picture her below, flipping it back and forth. "He carried this thing everywhere, like he was some investment banker or something. Remember how he'd type away at Chloe's soccer games? Sitting in the stands, just . . . pounding keys. I'd get so frustrated with him."

Huh. I don't remember that. I remember him cheering me on, not ignoring me for some email. Funny how two people can remember the same thing totally differently.

Mom shuffles, and it sounds like she's digging through the box more. "No charger, though. And . . . yep. It's dead. Thanks, Will."

The word *dead* hangs heavy over the moment. They're quiet, and the frogs and crickets sing.

Downstairs, Charlie squawks in her cage. We tried

to cover it so she'd sleep, but we don't have a blanket big enough to cover the whole cage and block out all the light. "Skull! Skull!" she shouts. Same as earlier. I sure wish I knew what she was saying. "Skull! Skull!"

Mom sighs. "Know a good chicken recipe?"

"Mom!" I shout through the window without getting up off my bed. "That's terrible!" I know she's joking, but *gah!*

"Sorry, honey. You're right. I was kidding, of course," Mom shouts up at me.

Grammy swats her with what sounds like a rolled-up magazine. "Teresa, you're awful!"

"Eighty years, Mom. *Eighty.*"

But that part makes me smile. Eighty years! Charlie and I will be lifelong pals. I picture me with gray hair, hunched over, using a walker with tennis balls on its feet, Charlie perched on the front like it's her own tiny pirate ship. Navigating old age together. We're going to live a long, long time, me and Charlie.

I swallow past a sudden lump in my throat. I wish Uncle Will had had that.

5

FEND FOR YOURSELF

Mom's declared it another "fend for yourself" night for dinner; she has a late meeting at work. Grammy's fixing herself a peanut butter and banana sandwich. Jacob is on his third bowl of Froot Loops. I'm digging around in the freezer, but nothing sounds good. Pizza rolls? Nope. Chicken fried rice? Nope. Mac and cheese? Ugh.

Something about eating a meal that no one else is eating feels . . . lonely?

I've perched Charlie on the light fixture above our kitchen island. She hangs on with one claw; with the other, she holds a chunk of corn on the cob and pecks at it. Half the corn makes it into her beak; the other half sprinkles across our stove.

Friendly eyes all this with a heavy dose of suspicion, but still leaps onto the counter and samples some of the dropped corn.

"Alexa, play Stevie Wonder," Charlie croaks, and sure enough, our tiny electronic tower lights up and begins to play "Superstitious." She bobs and weaves to the music, the light fixture swaying like a tiny swing. More corn falls.

Grammy, Jacob, and I are all frozen for a half beat, wide-eyed and silent, then we burst into laughter. "Dude, did Uncle Will teach you that?" Jacob reaches up, fist closed, like he's offering her a fist bump. She taps his knuckles lightly with her cob of corn.

Grammy stands on tiptoe to stroke a finger down Charlie's back. "Excellent taste in music, too."

I grin. "I have the smartest bird on the planet."

Suddenly, "fend for yourself" night feels less lonely. We all dance and bob and weave around the kitchen while Alexa cycles through Stevie Wonder songs. Friendly dashes out of the kitchen like it's on fire. We're all stomping and laughing, and the music is loud, so when Charlie squawks next, what I hear is, "By your side! By your side!"

It makes me grin even bigger. Eighty years, this bird and I will be pals. "By your side, Big C!" I shout.

"By your side!" Except Charlie's words sound more garbled this time, like maybe I misunderstood.

Something in my gut twists. "Alexa, volume down!" I shout.

Alexa turns down the music a half notch. Unnoticeable, really.

"By your side!"

"Alexa, off!" I shout. It's suddenly echoey silent, and Jacob raises an eyebrow at me. What a rip that he got the eyebrow-raising gene, too.

Charlie squawks again. It's not *by your side*.

"Sigh at night?" Jacob asks, looking between me and Grammy. "Is that what she's saying?"

"Sigh at night!" I nod. It does sound more like that. But . . . not?

Charlie flusters her feathers, like she's getting frustrated that we don't understand her. "Cyanide! Cyanide!" She drops her picked-over cob of corn. It plonks against the stove like a rock.

"Cyanide?" I say. We're crowded around Charlie now, looking up at her. She's silhouetted with the light behind her. She looks like a creepy crow.

Jacob shakes his head. "That's not even a word."

"It is," I whisper. "Cyanide. It's a type of poison."

A chill prickles the back of my neck.

Here's the thing: Grief can make your mind and your heart do weird things. Like when Will first told us he was sick, Grammy went and died her hair fuchsia. Brightest pink you ever saw. No one said a word about it, and then three weeks later, it was red again.

As much as we're all trying to move past grieving with our *go go go*, we're still here. Stuck in grief. Like fighting to get out of a sticky mud puddle. You only get more stuck.

"Poison," Grammy whispers. She's shaking her head. "That's ridiculous. There is no way that bird is saying *cyanide*."

"Cyanide!" Charlie echoes.

Jacob looks from Charlie to me to Grammy. "Maybe that's just her speaking British, you know? Maybe it means something different in that language."

Grammy sighs heavily and rolls her eyes. She pats Jacob on the elbow.

"Cyanide! Cyanide!"

I grab Grammy and Jacob by their wrists. I tell them about *skull* and *homicide de-trek-tive*. I feel queasy but certain. Absolutely certain. How else could Charlie know those words?

"Don't you see?" I say. "It all makes sense! Uncle Will . . . he was *poisoned*!"

Before Uncle Will passed away, his skin grew thin and papery gray. He dropped a ton of weight. He stopped coming around as much, and then not at all, and he told us not to visit, either. He was sick. The doctors told us it was a rare genetic disease. Was it?

He had been young and healthy before. It all happened so fast. Three months from the time he told us he was sick until . . .

Until I'm the one taking care of his bird.

Jacob's eyes grow hard and dark. "Poisoned? No way."

I suck in a shaky breath. "Yesterday Charlie said, 'It was murder.'"

As soon as I say it, Charlie repeats it: "It was murder. It was murder."

The three of us gasp and collectively take a step back, as if Charlie is the prime suspect.

We all eye the bird.

Grammy lifts her chin. "No. Chloe, your imagination is getting the better of you."

Jacob nods.

I know what I need to do. I need to get into Uncle Will's laptop. That's the first place they start in Grammy's true crime podcasts—the personal records. And Mom said it herself—he brought that thing everywhere. It was the only thing he ever checked to make sure he had before leaving, say, a coffee shop. I need to check his email, his bank account . . . but I need a charger to get the laptop to work.

I wonder why Cheatham the lawyer guy didn't grab the charger with the laptop when he cleaned out Will's apartment. Is he covering for someone?

Or was the charger *in the box*, and someone stole it to cover their tracks?

I gulp. "We need to make a list of suspects."

"Suspects!" Charlie shouts. She spreads her large wings—they're almost two feet across, as wide as Friendly from tip to tail—and sails down across the kitchen to my shoulder. Her claws dig through my T-shirt.

Grammy shakes her head once, abruptly, like she's waking up. Her shoulders drop. "No. Surely not. Chloe, honey. You've misunderstood."

My jaw tightens. I mean, Grammy is something like 112 years old. No way she heard Charlie correctly with her old ears. Plus, don't older folks get confused a lot? That bird said *cyanide*. That bird told us *it was murder*. That bird knew the word *suspects*.

On my shoulder, Charlie's feathers fluff, then settle. "Cheerio! Salad fork! Alexa, play Kiss!"

"Rock and Roll All Nite" blares through tiny speakers, and Charlie dances on my shoulder. We all look at each other suspiciously. I side-eye my brother and grandmother so hard, my eyeballs hurt. But I know *my* first suspect. It makes my heart hurt, but I know who should top the list. Who had access to that charger before any of us? Who got so angry when he didn't get what he wanted at the Will will reading? So when Jacob smirks and says, "C'mon. Everyone loved Uncle Will! Who would do something like that?" I pause before I whisper:

"Uncle Frank."

6

THE MATTRESS MAGIC MANATEE

My mind is whirling with how to investigate Will's murder. Recover the stolen charger. Get in his laptop. Make a list of suspects. Investigate each one. Check, check, check.

But until then . . .

"Jake, you don't have practice tonight, do you?"

Jacob smirks at me. "No. Why?"

"We need to set up surveillance outside Uncle Frank's house."

Jacob smashes his lips together. "Like a campout?"

I glance at Grammy, who can't help but shake her head at Jacob and his many Jacobisms. "A *stakeout*," I say. "Yep, exactly."

"C'mon, Chlo. No way Uncle Frank did this."

I narrow my gaze at him. I know how to get him to do what I want. "Are you afraid of what you're gonna find out?"

We lock eyes for the next few moments before Jacob throws his hands in the air. "Jeez. Okay, Chloe. You're making a mistake here. And you're paying me for gas."

He grabs his keys and his wallet. "Listen, Squeak. I'm only doing this to clear Uncle Frank's name, got it? No way Uncle Will was . . . murdered." His voice catches on that last word. That surprises me. I know Jacob misses Uncle Will, too, of course, but he doesn't get emotional much.

I run to my room and jam a backpack full of spy stuff: My phone. Binoculars. A bottle of water. An empty bottle, in case . . . well, bathroom. Not sure how that'd work exactly, but it's what they do in the movies. A fresh spiral notebook and a purply sparkle pen. I dash back downstairs and hesitate before I extend my arm out to Charlie. She hops on board. "Charlie's coming, too. She knows the clues."

"That bird poops in my car and you're paying to have it detailed."

Based on what I've seen from Charlie so far, she will absolutely poop in Jacob's car. I toss a packet of baby wipes into the backpack, too.

Jacob bangs out of the house. I start to follow, but Grammy slides in front of me, her big jewelry clanging. Her eyes are glassy with tears.

"Don't try to talk me out of this, Grammy," I say. My voice wavers but I jut my chin in the air.

Grammy shakes her head and then pulls me into a tight hug. "I won't, sweetie," she says into my hair. "I understand that for some reason, you *need* to do this. So I'm not going to stop you. But listen. Don't tell your mother. She'd *freak*." Grammy squeezes me once more. She smells like Jergens lotion and a tinge of smoke.

Outside, Jacob is already halfway up the block. "Where are you parked?" I ask as I catch up to him, scanning the cars that constantly line both sides of our street.

"Far," he grumbles. He jerks his head back over his shoulder to Grammy's car, parked in our driveway. "I don't know why she always gets the driveway spot. She leaves the house, like, once a week."

"Dude, she's ancient," I say, huffing to keep up with Jacob's pace. It's harder to jog with a parrot perched on my shoulder. "Let her have the parking spot."

"You'll see when you get a car," he says. "It sucks parking on the street so far away."

We half jog in silence for another three blocks before Jacob's orange Camaro comes into view. He grins at it like he's greeting a girlfriend or a dog. When we sidle up to it, Jacob huffs a breath on the hood and buffs off a speck with the sleeve of his hoodie.

I swing open the low, heavy door and duck inside. It's odd, balancing Charlie and doing this.

"It's okay," Charlie croaks as we duck into the hot, dark car. "It's all good. All good." She whistles a little tune, like she's working up her bravery. I realize that to her, this is a strange car.

"You're okay, Charlie," I say, and stroke her soft, downy head. "You're okay."

"You're okay," she echoes. I grin.

Jacob carefully folds the shiny silver sunscreen he had splayed across his windshield. Something about this flusters Charlie, and she squawks, then hops off my shoulder and around the car—headrest, back seat, headrest, dashboard—all while cawing and flapping and leaving a tornado of feathers everywhere. And— yep. Poop. I swipe it up quickly, hoping Jake didn't see.

"Do NOT let that bird tear my pleather seats!" Jacob shouts, which just gets Charlie worked up more. And hey, I get it. This car is Jacob's prized possession. Since he was thirteen, he spent every hour he wasn't at school or football practice twirling sale signs for the Mattress Magic store down the street. He'd put on this gross frumpy gray costume, put in some earbuds, and dance near the intersection to lure customers in. He was so good at sign twirling that the store kept giving him raises and begging him to stay on. They wanted him to become their permanent sign-twirling mascot, the Mattress Magic Manatee. But the moment he raised enough money for his dream car, he hung up the manatee suit and retired from sign twirling.

I finally get Charlie to calm down by directing the air-conditioning vent at her. She hops onto my lap and places her face right against the vent, letting the cool air ruffle her feathers. I wonder if that's what flying feels like. I wonder if she misses flying with her clipped wings. I know I would.

I get a whiff of something from the vents, and my face curls. "Your car smells like Taco Bell."

Jacob smiles. "Thanks!"

"It's not a compliment."

Jacob swerves into traffic, Beastie Boys blaring from the radio. Charlie dances, bobbing up and down, lifting one foot and then the other like she's doing tiny rocker kicks. She whistles and clicks throughout the song.

"She is a cool bird," Jacob says with a grin.

"Yeah, she is," I say.

"Pretty bird!" Charlies caws.

We laugh. "Okay, you're pretty, too," I say.

We drive in silence for a bit, then Jacob says, "Chlo,

listen. I gotta ask. You really think Uncle Will was murdered?" His voice isn't doing a very good job of masking what he feels: he thinks I'm nuts.

Yes. No? I don't know how to answer that. Uncle Will was definitely too healthy and young to die. Too . . . *good*. Like, how does something so terrible happen to someone so great? So I say, "If he was, I want to find out who did it. Don't you?"

Jacob shrugs—not a yes, not a no. "It's not Uncle Frank, though."

"That's why we need to get into Uncle Will's laptop!" I say, a little too loud and fast. Charlie glares at me for disturbing her air bath. "Just like in Grammy's podcasts—they always check the laptop first. I know we'll find what we're looking for there. I know what we find will lead us to his killer."

I pause. "And don't you think it's suspicious his charger is missing?"

Jacob smirks as he glances in the rearview mirror. "Missing? What do you mean? It just wasn't in the box."

"Or was it?" I ask, trying in vain to cock an eyebrow. I shake off the attempt. "Was it there before the will reading, and now it's missing? We all know who had access to that box of goodies before the rest of us."

"Uncle Frank?" Jacob says. He swerves around a

person on an electric scooter. "He couldn't have—I mean—we were all there. We would've seen him."

I suppress a grin. "Oh, but you know Uncle Frank's special talent. . . ."

Jacob mashes his lips together. His cheeks redden. "Chloe, don't."

"I mean, he *is* highly trained in sleight of hand . . ."

"Chloe, *stop*!"

I chuckle, but I'm also serious. "Uncle Frank is a *magician*, Jacob." Jake winces when I say the word. "He could've snuck that charger right out of the box without any of us seeing. Easily. Because . . . you know . . . the *magic*."

Jacob huffs loudly. "It was a terrible phase of his, but he's over it now."

"Is he?" I ask. Dang, this whole conversation is full of moments where I could really use that one-eyebrow-raised thing. "Or do you just have bad memories of being sawn in half as his assistant?"

That does it. Jacob *hates* being reminded of the times Uncle Frank convinced him to wear a sparkly unitard and serve as his magician's assistant. Jacob was only nine at the time, but the pictures are *priceless*. Blackmail gold, the kind of thing I can't wait to show every future girlfriend of his. Jacob frogs my arm—a direct hit—without taking his eyes off the road.

"Ow-uh!" I say, grinning. I turn serious quick, though. "But honestly. Uncle Frank could've taken the charger, and you know it. He's good, Jake. And he's trying to cover his tracks, I bet."

I think it's cool that Uncle Frank is a magician. He does little tricks all the time—the pulling-a-quarter-from-behind-your-ear sort of thing. He hasn't done that in a while, though, now that I think about it. He stopped right about the time we found out Uncle Will was really sick.

We fall silent. Uncle Frank lives across Charleston, in a swanky Mount Pleasant neighborhood. The houses slowly become bigger, the lawns greener, the cars shinier.

Jacob turns to me at a stoplight. "What if he doesn't have it, Squeak? What then?"

"We could buy a new charger," I say. But I already know how Jacob's going to respond.

"For that old clunker? If you can find one, a charger for that ancient thing would be like eighty dollars," he says. "No way Mom will buy one of those."

"Yeah . . ."

His eyes soften. It's weird to go from arm punches to pity in just a few moments. "I could put in a good word for you at Mattress Magic if you want? You could make eighty dollars there in about three weeks."

"Three weeks?! That seems like a long time for

Will's killer to be on the loose."

Jacob blows a bubble with the gum he's chewing, and it pops loudly. "If you don't find the old one, then it's no charger. No laptop."

I nod. "Yep, okay. I guess I can put on a lumpy manatee suit for that."

Jacob laughs. "You want to talk about things that smell like Taco Bell? That suit totally reeks! My boss used to say it was fart-soaked!"

I gag. So disgusting. Sounds like a lot to endure, but it *is* to find a murderer.

Charlie cocks her head next to the air vent. "Ta-CO Bell! Taco BELL!" She's trying out these new words, rolling them around in her tiny bird beak, and Jacob and I laugh as we slide up to Uncle Frank's house for our campout. Erm . . . *stakeout*.

7

YOU MEDDLING KIDS

Uncle Frank's house looks like a museum and a library rolled into one. It's got all these fancy columns and swirly details hanging off it. And it's painted light blue, Charleston blue, the color of sky and sea. "The color of money," Mom said when he first painted the house. Palm trees and palmetto trees and wisteria vines are everywhere, and the grass looks like it was trimmed with toenail clippers, it's so precise.

Uncle Frank is rich. Like, so rich that we—Mom, Grammy, Jacob, Will, and I—never discuss how rich he is, because Grammy thinks money talk like that is "vulgar." Uncle Frank invented some kind of app that helps credit card companies do something. Mom says the harder the job is to describe, the more money it pays.

Which is why it takes three weeks to make $80 as a manatee, I guess.

We park across the wide street from Uncle Frank's home. His house is surrounded by a tall iron fence with a huge gate, but with the binoculars I brought, I can see the massive carved front door from here. I watch it for ten or fifteen minutes when I realize I've had just about enough of not sleeping till Brooklyn and I change the radio. "Taylor Swift, yes!"

"Nope," Jacob says, switching it back. "I love Tay-Tay as much as the next guy, but we need some heavy-rocking tunes to stay awake on this campout."

I change it back. "*Stake*out, Jay, and that's why we need quieter music. We don't need—"

A knock on the window next to me makes me leap in my seat, which makes Charlie squawk and fluster like she's trying to fly again. She hits her head on the car ceiling and drops into my lap. "Charlie!"

But she shakes it off, beak to tail tip, like a dog shaking off water. "All is well!" she says in her awful British accent.

In the window is Uncle Frank, holding up a bag of Twizzlers and a huge carton of Goldfish crackers.

"Uncle F!" Jacob shouts with a smile. He unlocks the car doors, and Uncle Frank climbs into the back seat.

Jacob rips into the Twizzlers like a hyena rips into

the corpse of a zebra. "Thanks for the snacks!"

"Grammy told you we were coming, didn't she?" I grumble.

Uncle Frank looks guilty. "Well, yeah."

Jacob tears into another red licorice stick and Uncle Frank gently offers Charlie a Goldfish. I'm happy to say that Charlie's loyalties are intact; she eyes the cracker suspiciously and then looks at me like she's asking if we should trust him.

Why is no one taking any of this seriously? I feel like a gurgling red lava lamp inside, churning and hot. I take myself by surprise and blurt out: "Where were you on the night of March twenty-seventh?"

March 27. The night Uncle Will died.

Uncle Frank looks hurt, but then his face softens. "March twenty-seventh. I was at the hospital with Will. He had just been admitted the day before, remember? Your mom and Grammy were there too."

I feel a lump swell in my throat, and I blink to hold back tears. Of course I knew that. The hospital wouldn't let me and Jacob in to see Uncle Will; they told us we were "too young." That part stung worse than a blistering sunburn.

Why am I being so weird lately?

Uncle Frank reaches forward, as if to place his hand on my shoulder, but Charlie pecks at it and he pulls it away. Good bird.

"Did you take Uncle Will's laptop charger? Do you have access to cyanide? You wouldn't really kill your brother, would you?"

That last question hangs there in the air, ugly and stinking like cigar smoke. I almost gag on the thought.

"Chloe," he says softly from the back seat, "I'm sorry you're so upset. I hate that you're feeling this way. Grief . . . *phew*," Uncle Frank huffs. His eyes redden suddenly. "Grief makes you act in ways you wouldn't normally act. It makes you point fingers and try to place blame. I mean, look—I was so mad that Will called this silly bird his best friend, on top of all the other stunts he pulled right before he died . . . well, I lost it. I've been trying to be my big brother's best friend for years."

We sit in silence for a minute, until Charlie calls out, "Hi, Will! Hello! Hello!"

I laugh through my tears, the whole car swimming. I face Uncle Frank. "Why are you being so nice? You're not supposed to be this calm when someone accuses you of murder."

Uncle Frank clears his throat, apparently swallowing tears, too. "Oh! Right. Um . . . Okay, how's this? DANG IT, CHLOE—"

"Nope," I interrupt with a laugh. "No murderer ever said 'dang it.'"

Jacob grins and points his Twizzler at Uncle Frank. "Agree."

"Right, right. Okay. Um . . . How's this? I would've gotten away with this if it weren't for you meddling kids!"

"Ha!" I burst out laughing and swipe a tear off my cheek. "You're not seriously dropping Scooby-Doo on me now, are you?"

We all laugh, but it quickly dwindles. Uncle Frank munches on some Goldfish. Charlie finally accepts one from him, and she crunches it whole. I scoot cracker bits under the seat with the toe of my sneaker before Jacob sees.

"I tell you what," I say, twisting in my seat to fully face Uncle Frank. "You're not off my suspects list *yet*. But if you help me find Uncle Will's killer, that'll prove your innocence for sure."

Charlie ruffles her wings and stretches a claw forward. "Find the killer! Find the killer! It was poison. *AWWWK!*"

A bird voice sounds extra-large and extra-loud in a small car. We all slide our eyes at each other. *See?* I want to shout. *I'm not crazy!*

Uncle Frank inhales deeply. "Okay. I'll help. I'll help you with this investigation, Chloe."

I notice that he doesn't say, *I'll help you find Will's killer, Chloe*, so he doesn't quite believe me. But hey. I'll take what I can get.

Jacob huffs loudly, throws his head back against

his headrest, and rolls his eyes. "I'm in, too, if Uncle Frank is."

I clap and squeal and bounce in my seat, Charlie bobbing around on my knees. "Thank you, guys."

Uncle Frank hugs me awkwardly from the back seat. "Of course. And listen—I'm not telling you to keep secrets from your mom or anything, but y'all. If she knew about this? She would *freak*."

"We know," Jacob and I say in harmony.

"We know! We know!" Charlie echoes.

Uncle Will starts to climb out of the back seat and pauses. "Why are you looking for Will's laptop charger?"

Jacob points his thumb at me. "Sherlock here thinks that we can find evidence in his laptop. Someone who wanted to, you know . . ." He slashes his hand across his throat and makes a gagging sound, his tongue sticking out. I whack his arm.

"Grammy's true crime podcasts," I say. "The investigators always start with the victim's computer."

"Victim!" Charlie sings. "Pretty girl." Man, can that bird creep me out!

Uncle Frank unfolds himself out of the car and stands on the sidewalk. He strokes his chin. "It's a good place to start."

I beam. Jacob scowls. "But you don't have the charger?" Jacob asks.

Uncle Frank shrugs and looks a bit sheepish. "If it wasn't in that box, I don't know where it would be. I honestly didn't look too closely at the contents. I mean, Robin Hood?!"

I chuckle. Robin Hood. Classic Uncle Will.

Uncle Frank's jaw shifts. He's chewing on an idea. "Will brought that laptop everywhere the last few years. Teresa and I used to tease him all the time about it, because he never actually had a job where he needed to, you know, stay on top of email or anything."

Jacob nods. "So that charger could be anywhere, is what you're saying."

"Yep," Uncle Frank says. "I guess I could buy another one. Will's laptop was *old*, though. Thing was a brick. We'll have to special order a new charger, most likely. But it would be interesting to know where the original one is, you know?"

"Might be a clue," I say. And yeah, I know how dorky that sounds.

Uncle Frank taps on the hood of Jake's car, and we pull away from the curb.

We drive home in silence, Charlie curled under her wing in the back seat. I tumble the possibilities through my head: Where would Uncle Will work on his laptop? His apartment, of course. The library. A park. The ice cream parlor. . . .

"That coffee shop!" I shout.

Jacob's eyes widen. "Yeah! The one where Will's ex-girlfriend used to work! Kaley?"

"Kiley," I correct him. I try to picture her, but the memory is fuzzy. We only met her a handful of times. She was nice. Loved anime. That's about all I can recall. "What was the name of that place?"

Jacob pauses, shrugs. "No clue. But that was a really messy breakup, remember?"

For some reason, a tiny flare of anger erupts in me. How does Jacob know that Uncle Will's breakup was messy, and I don't? "No," I say.

"I mean, it's always the jilted lover, right?" Jacob switches lanes and turns, and I hang on to the Oh No bar overhead.

"It's always the *butler*," I mutter, but Jacob doesn't hear me. I chuckle to myself; the thought of Uncle Will with a butler! He'd make a butler do things like juggle crawfish shells and dance the Macarena.

"Yep. I'm sure it was Kaley," Jacob says.

My lips flatten. "*Kiley*," I repeat. "But you're right. It can't hurt to check her out. Let's add her to the list."

I dig my notebook and purple glitter pen from my backpack. Underneath *Uncle Frank* on the page labeled *Suspects!*, I add *Kiley the ex-girlfriend*.

That night, I finally take Dad's advice. I decide to start recording my memories of Uncle Will, the snapshots that flitter through my thoughts all day like moths. I like writing down lists and small ideas and doodles, but these snapshots, they feel too big and quick to write down. Like I can't write fast enough to capture them fully before they fly away again. So, I'm going to use my voice recorder app.

I push the large red Record button.

"Uh, hi. Is this thing on? Huh." Stupid joke. "I, uh . . . yeah. So I'm thinking of this one time, we all went to Charleston pier and sat on the big porch swings that hang under the dock. I was maybe . . . five or six? It was so nice and peaceful—we were watching the sun set and I remember thinking, *This is a perfect day*.

"It's wild, but if I close my eyes, I can still feel all the little details of that day. We'd had ice cream, so my forearms were sticky and gritty. The air was salty, and the sun was hot. The chains on the porch swing squeaked and moaned as we rocked back and forth. But then we started swinging really high—as high as a porch swing can go, at least—and my heart pounded, and my stomach dropped, and I gripped the handrest. Then Uncle Will leapt off the swing at the highest point and tumbled through the sand. It took my breath away, watching him fly.

"'Y'all do it, too!' he yelled back to me and Jake. Mom was on another swing nearby, eating her ice cream cone. 'Nope! Don't listen to your uncle! No broken bones, please!'

"'Do it!' he yelled. 'Nope!' she yelled. Oh man, she was so mad at him. Her face was bright red, and it wasn't from sunburn.

"Jacob jumped. He landed and his feet slipped out from under him and he plowed face first into the sand, but he laughed and laughed. I was too scared to jump. Mom told me I didn't have to, but I wanted to, so bad. I wanted to be like Jacob and Uncle Will. So I leapt off that swing. I still remember the feeling; arms and legs flailing and pumping through the sky, hitting the soft, hot beach with my bare feet, tumbling and rolling and getting a mouthful of sand. I landed on a shell. It hurt. I started to cry. But Jacob and Uncle Will pulled me up, dusted me off, and clapped me on the back. 'You did it!' 'Awesome, Squeak!' THAT part felt great. I did it! I spit out sand and stopped crying.

"Mom was so mad, she had to walk away down the beach, while Grammy lit into Will."

I turn off the voice recorder.

So, yeah. I think Uncle Frank is right. As much as I hate it, we can't tell Mom about this investigation. She really would freak.

8

I LOVE YOU. BYE BYE.

Grammy listens to this true crime podcast called *WHODUNNIT?* As it turns out, we all end up listening to it, too, because Grammy says her old ears don't "take to" earbuds, so she blares the podcast wherever she is. You can do that when you're 116 years old, I guess. The theme song bops through my head now as I'm bumping along in the school bus the Monday after our stakeout:

> *Whoooodunnit?*
> *A stranger, a friend, someone ushered him to*
> THE END.
> *Some family, a peer, who kept her from*

another year?
WHOOOOOODUNNIT?

My breath fogs the thin window. I write in the mist with my fingertip: *WHODUNNIT?*

Both Grammy and Uncle Frank warned me that Mom would freak if she knew I was trying to find out WHODUNNIT. Which, okay—maybe not my smartest choice ever, trying to sniff out a killer. A chill chases down my spine at that word. But I have to know! I mean, this is *Uncle Will*. Awesome, wonderful, perfect Uncle Will. And when did Mom become this person who freaks out so often? I remember her just a few years ago—snapshot! Her and Will hunched over, hands on knees, laughing until they cried while they tossed long streamers of toilet paper into the trees next door for the neighbor's fiftieth birthday. Why isn't she still like that? What happened?

"Earth to Chloe!" Audrey taps me on the knee. "Come in, Chloe! Did you hear what I said? Coach Reynolds canceled soccer practice today. His daughter's turned into a rhinoceros, and they have to perform emergency surgery to remove the horn."

"Hmmm. That's too bad." I squeak my fingertip through the WHODUNNIT message so Audrey doesn't see and think I'm losing it.

Am I losing it?

Audrey laughs. "What *are* you thinking about today? You're in a total fog!"

I snap awake. No *way* I'm telling my friends about all this. They're awesome, but how do you even start that conversation? *Well, I'm distracted because I'm investigating my uncle's murder. Right now the two suspects are his brother and his ex.* Nope. I might as well tell them I've decided to colonize Mars.

"I . . . uh . . . what do you think Ms. Umar will assign next? I hope we move on from painting sometime soon."

Audrey shakes her head. "Lindsey says she sticks with painting the rest of the year." Audrey's older sister Lindsey is a year ahead of us in school, and she takes great pleasure in letting us know all the terrible things that lie ahead.

"Painting is just so . . . *messy*! The colors are so beautiful until they mush together and get all muddy and gross and it's so hard to know how to finish the painting!" For some reason, my throat tightens as I'm saying this. I blink back sting. It's confusing when weird emotions bubble to the surface like this. And it happens so often lately.

Audrey's face softens and she squeezes my hand. "Well, no soccer practice today. You can take as long as you'd like with your . . . painting?"

• • •

Charlie flaps her wings when I walk in the house after school, and it's like getting a big wave hello. "Bye! Goodbye! Bye bye!" she says, then whistles and clicks. Charlie knows that the door opening and closing goes with *hello* and *goodbye*, but she doesn't always get them in the right order. I laugh.

"Goodbye, Charlie." I scritch her head, then offer her some lettuce and the crook of my arm. She hops on board, and we head to our family computer, on a desk in the living room. She's plucked out more feathers today, and new bumpy pink skin shows underneath. I hope soon she'll feel less stressed, more a part of this family.

I can't remember Kiley's last name, and I don't get very far on social media without it. Uncle Will isn't friends with her on Facebook anymore, so that's a dead end.

Lots of friends have written on Will's Facebook page. Things like:

Tons of good memories, bud. RIP.
Up there playing a mean air guitar, I just know it.
Miss you, big guy. You were one of the good ones.

I slam the laptop shut.

It's kinda hard to hunt for a murderer when you

don't want to remember that a person is dead.

Charlie plucks at my hair. It hurts, but I don't stop her. "Pretty girl. Cowabunga." Then she blows a raspberry. "*Pbbbbfffttt.* I love you. Bye bye."

"Yep, Charlie." I tap the closed laptop. "That's it exactly. I love you. Bye bye."

In the quiet of my bedroom, I press the red Record button on my voice memos app.

"After every soccer practice, Uncle Will was supposed to take me to dinner. But he never did—instead we went to Shakey's Ice Cream Parlor and got big scoops of ice cream. I got the same thing every time—mint chocolate chip. Uncle Will never got the same thing twice. He said he wanted to taste the whole wide world of ice cream. 'There's too many flavors out there just waiting for our taste buds, Chlo-dog!' he'd say. 'I want to taste every flavor the world has to offer.' He had this old, beat-up list of all the flavors Shakey's makes, and he checked off each one after he tried it."

I pause here. "Kiley would come sometimes. He'd always ask if it was okay for her to join us. What was I going to say? 'No, this is OUR time'? And she was nice. She'd laugh as he described the flavors: 'Nutty, with a rum aftertaste. Full-bodied and robust.' He gave each flavor a rating, too, between one and ten. Pistachio got an eight. Rum raisin—blech! A two. Christmas cookie—the only perfect ten. I wonder if that list is in Uncle Frank's box of stuff?"

I think for a moment. "I'd like to find it. I don't know how far he got on the list. I just know he didn't finish. Those ice cream dinners—they stopped when everything else stopped, right after the beginning of the year. One day he just never showed up for practice, and then he never showed up again. Which meant no more ice cream for dinner. He never told me why. He just quit on me."

9

OBSESSED

I'm a bit obsessed with finding Kiley. The next day at school, I add the Facebook app to my phone like a Boomer. I sneak peeks at it throughout the day, but I'm not much closer to finding her. Until I remember that Uncle Frank could be friends with her, too, right? They all hung out together—Uncle Will, Uncle Frank, Kiley. The bell rings just as I think this, and off I go to art.

Ms. Umar stands in front of the class in a gorgeous green-and-yellow wrap dress and matching headdress, her gold hoop earrings framing her face. Her smile feels like sitting in a slant of sunshine.

"Artists!" she says, clapping her hands. "I'm so excited for this next assignment, because we are painting"—she drums on the tops of her legs like a drumroll—"still lifes!"

It's like crickets are chirping, it's so quiet. I try to smile back at Ms. Umar, because she's so excited about this, but I can feel my cheeks fake-stretching. Gah—more painting!

Ms. Umar says, "Remember what Aristotle said, class. 'The aim of art is not to represent the outward appearance of things, but their inward significance.' That's what painting still lifes is all about." She's bouncing on her toes as she talks about still life painting being an "interplay of shadows and light, shape and form . . ."

My phone is practically shouting at me from my pocket: *Come find Kiley! You're so close!* So while Ms. Umar is writing things on the whiteboard about still life painting, I sneak it out.

Facebook . . . Uncle Frank . . . trying to find his profile . . .

"Chloe, no phones, ma'am. Bring it here, please." I look up from my lap. Ms. Umar is frowning at me, and it's like the sun has moved behind storm clouds. The whole class eyes me. I walk to the front of the room and put my phone in a shoebox on Ms. Umar's desk. She's decorated it to read *PHONES KILL BEAUTY*.

Now I am paying attention. I have to paint. Again.

Like, some fruit? Isn't that what still lifes are? And I do want a good grade on this. I love *making* things. Creating things. Sharing how I see things.

I have a snapshot moment: Uncle Will and me standing in the shadow of a statue called *Confederate Defenders of Charleston* on Oyster Point. It's two fellows—one holding a sword and shield, one holding a bundle of laurel. Uncle Will soaked in art like sand soaks in the rising tide, but there, he was silent. Anger sharpened his face, and he shook his head at last.

Can you imagine having as much talent as this artist did, and using it to glorify war and hate?

Art is big and important.

My fingers itch to push the big red button on my voice recorder app so I can capture that memory.

After class, I approach Ms. Umar's desk. "Ms. Umar, I'm so sorry I was on my phone in class." I am, too. I never want to be rude to my teachers. Especially not Ms. Umar.

Ms. Umar places my phone in my hands. "This isn't like you, Chloe. Is something going on?"

A murder? I think. I shiver and shake my head. "No, ma'am."

Ms. Umar's face shifts thoughtfully. "I'm sorry to do this, but you know the rules. No phones in class, period. I have to give you After School Service, do you understand? And I will need to call your mother to let her know why you're staying after school."

Please don't call my mom, I beg silently. *Not for an After School Service. If you do, I'll for sure be gr—*

"Grounded!" I shout aloud. I blink and burn with embarrassment.

"Excuse me?" Ms. Umar says, her eyebrows knit together.

"I . . . uh . . . I'm more *grounded* than this, Ms. Umar. More . . . centered. I know better than to look at my phone in class. It's rude, and I'm sorry."

She suppresses a grin. "Okay, Chloe. Thank you. But you're still getting After School Service."

Ms. Umar looks at me funny because of my huge smile. I practically skip out of her classroom because I've remembered:

Grounded! That's the name of the coffee shop in the Westside neighborhood where Kiley works. It's called *Grounded*.

10

REGRET IS A POISON, TOO

It's like I have a pantsload of bees—that's how jittery I am as I head to the vice principal's office to get my After School Service assignment. I'm not nervous for the reason you'd think: being in trouble like this. Nope, instead I'm jittery because I want to be looking up the location of Grounded. I want to beg Grammy or Jacob for a ride over there. I want to find *clues*.

School is really cramping my style these days.

I huff my bangs off my forehead. I've never been given After School Service before. My school has done away with traditional detention, which was just sitting and staring at four walls. Instead, they do this thing—After School Service—where you get assigned to a teacher for an afternoon (or several, if your misdeeds were terrible enough, but mine's just one day). The kids all refer to After School Service by its initials, which gets the teachers all worked up. Anyway, at After School Service, you help the teacher do whatever they ask. I've heard of kids having to do everything from testing a bin full of markers to see which ones are dried out to scraping gum off the bottom of the bleachers. I lift a quick prayer that *this* misdeed warrants a dried-out-marker type of detail.

And when I get my After School Service assignment, the irony just about kills me. Our library is reshelving books by genre (fantasy, sci-fi, manga, etc.) and Ms. Rollins, our librarian, asks me to put stickers on all the mystery books. They're little labels that wrap around the spine; each has a small magnifying glass on it to show that the book is a mystery. (Do I need a magnifying glass in my spy backpack? Maybe . . . all detectives seem to have one. Where does one even get a magnifying glass? Amazon Prime?)

The mystery books! I can't believe it. They have titles like *The Strangers* and *We Were Liars* and *One of Us Is Lying*. Is Kiley a liar? A killer? I shudder, even though the library is flooded with warm afternoon light. Uncle Will loved mysteries, especially Agatha Christie. He'd highlight her stories and break them apart scene by scene. *Masterful!* he'd shout, smiling and circling a paragraph in red ink. Snapshot! I don't think I can whip out my voice recorder in this quiet library to record this memory. But I smile.

"You're telling me I'm on the right path here, right, Uncle Will?" I murmur to the stained ceiling, then look around to make sure no one's seen me talking to my dead uncle. I wrap another tiny magnifying glass sticker around a book titled, coincidentally, *The Inheritance Games*. Me and Charlie, my inheritance, solving mysteries side by side. My gut clenches like a strong fist.

I know I'm on the right path.

"Are you kidding? I'm not taking you to Grounded." That afternoon, Grammy looks at me like I have two heads. And Jacob is at football practice, so Grammy's all I got.

"But—"

"No, Chloe. I'm not indulging this . . . *murder* theory of yours." Grammy licks her teeth. She's irked, but she takes a deep, calming breath. "How about we have ice cream, huh? It's been a while since we've made a banana split."

Been a while in this house now means *before Will died*. We both know it's our new timeline. "Okay," I huff. I can't wait until I can drive and investigate murders on my own.

Grammy gets out the bananas. Strawberry ice

cream. Chocolate syrup. Whipped cream. Sprinkles.

Okay, maybe this isn't such a bad idea after all.

As we assemble our monstrous banana splits, I scatter some rainbow sprinkles across the kitchen counter. Charlie hops off my elbow and starts pecking at them. I giggle.

Grammy quirks an eyebrow at me. "Is Charlie supposed to eat that?"

I shrug. "Probably not. But neither should we."

"Fair point."

We're silent for a bit, except for moans of *yummmm* and *mmmhmmm* between bites of ice cream. And then I can't take it anymore.

"Grammy, why won't you bring me to Grounded? I mean, it can't hurt anything, right? Just to poke around? Ask Kiley if she has Uncle Will's laptop charger?"

Grammy sets her spoon down. "Chloe. Honey. I'm just not ready. How do I . . . ?" She inhales deeply. "Look. I'm still coming to terms with how I left things with Will." She swallows, hard. Her eyes glass over. It's not often I see Grammy look this vulnerable.

"What do you mean?" I say this to the ice cream, not to Grammy. Because I think I might I feel the same way.

Grammy clears her throat. Her voice comes out high and tight: "Bug, I was Will's *mother*. I *am* his mother.

And I didn't see the signs! Why didn't I see how sick he was? When he was pulling away from all of us—why didn't I know what that meant? Why didn't I demand to know what was going on?!" A single tear works its way down Grammy's cheek.

I blink back sting, but this confirms what I believe. "Grammy . . . what if . . . *whew*. What if there weren't signs of sickness because he wasn't sick? Because he was poisoned?"

That word, *poisoned*, hangs over us like a storm cloud. Suddenly my banana split is too sweet. My stomach roils. I screech my chair back and dump the bowl loudly in the kitchen sink.

I lift Charlie onto my arm, stomp up the stairs, slam my door, place her on my desk, and fling myself on the bed. I whip out my voice recorder. Snapshot!

"Regret is a poison, too," I say into my phone. "NONE of us saw the signs. That means something, right?" I'm practically shouting into my phone. "It means something that none of Uncle Will's family even knew he was really sick. He wouldn't have kept us ALL in the dark. He would've told us. He would've told ME!"

I swallow past the dry lump in my throat. "After the new year, he started pulling away from all of us. He canceled on me, on coaching my indoor soccer league.

Really left us in a lurch. He made Mom so angry. Grammy, too—they had to cancel stuff and move stuff around because he was just one big NO-SHOW."

Charlie squawks and flutters her wings, likely because I'm really worked up now. "He didn't show up for any of us! He missed Jacob in *Fiddler on the Roof*. He missed Mom's birthday dinner. He missed Uncle Frank getting that award from the food bank. He bailed on us all. We were so pissed at him!"

I'm grinding my teeth now, remembering this. Charlie paces and plucks a few feathers from under her wing. "And then! Out of nowhere, over my spring break, he suddenly decides he wants to take me to Folly Beach? To swing through McDonald's and grab a Shamrock Shake? WHO DOES THAT?" I shout into the recorder, my voice breaking. My heart breaking.

"I was so done. Now, suddenly, he wants to hang out?! So I told him no."

I take a deep, shaky breath.

"And a week later, he was gone."

11

GROUNDED

"Five thirty in the morning, Chloe." Jacob lays his head on his steering wheel. We sit in his car, waiting for Grounded to open.

"I know what time it is, Jacob."

"Say it with me: it is five thirty in the morning."

"I'm not saying it with you."

"It's still dark out."

"Yep."

"It's so *eeeeeaaarrrrrlyyyyy*."

"Your whining is making it worse."

"Okay, Mom."

"Speaking of Mom"—I shift, and the pleather seat squeaks—"do you think she bought your story? You know, of why we had to leave the house so early this morning? She's still mad at me for getting After School Service."

Jacob chuckles. "After School Service. *Chlo-eee got in trou-ble!*" he sings.

I roll my eyes at him.

He shrugs. "I think so. I mean, technically, I didn't lie. I told her I've been worried about you, and I wanted to take you out for a coffee before school." He studies his fingernails. "She actually got a little teary and hugged me and it was primo awkwardo."

My forehead wrinkles. "But you're not really worried about me?"

Jacob yawns too loudly and stretches too big. "Five-freaking-thirty a.m.!"

I huff. "There's no other time to come here, Jay. You know that. We had to squeeze it in before school. I just hope Kiley works the morning shift. And, you know, knows something about Will's laptop charger."

Which gives me the idea to text Uncle Frank: **You bought a charger for Will's laptop yet?**

He responds almost immediately, which doesn't surprise me too much. Uncle Frank, awake at 5:30 a.m.? Not surprising. Uncle Will, awake at 5:30 a.m.? The only reason he'd be up that early is if he never went to bed.

No, Chloe, not yet, Uncle Frank's reply reads. I can hear how irked he is in this text. **It's not been the highest item on my priority list. Patience, Bug.**

Patience? When there's a killer on the loose? I bet Miss Marple was never told to chill out. I fling myself back against the passenger seat.

The lights inside Grounded flicker on at last, and hallelujah, there's Kiley unlocking the door. We pile out of Jacob's car. Kiley's hair is different than I remember—it's bright blue now—and as we get closer, I can see the back of her hand is covered in a new tattoo—an infinity symbol. She's holding a phone to her ear, and when she turns, I catch a flash of a new nose ring. Grammy's podcast says people often change things about their appearance when they feel guilty.

When Jacob and I enter, she's already behind the counter, her back turned toward the door. We can't help but overhear her conversation:

"No, no," she says, wedging the phone between her ear and her shoulder. "Lavinia Fisher was hanged, remember? Correct. Not to be confused with the Gray Man. The one killed by a tree. *Supposedly*. Gotta keep 'em all straight... ha!" Kiley picks up a huge knife and slams it through a lemon. She listens to her phone a moment longer before saying, "Yes. She's the one who fell into a coma."

Jacob's eyes widen. He grabs my wrist, tight, and starts to back up, pulling me with him.

We're almost to the door when Kiley catches a glimpse of us in the shiny chrome of the espresso machine.

"Oh!" she says, startled. She fumbles her phone, and it crashes to the floor. As she scrambles to pick it up, Jacob and I make a messy push toward the door. We're almost safely outside when Kiley says, "Chloe? Jacob?"

Jacob and I turn to face her. She's still holding the knife. We eye each other. My voice sounds like I'm talking through a spinning fan when I say, "Hi, Kiley."

"Call you back," Kiley says into the phone, and she hangs up. That can't be good. I hear Jacob gulp.

"You two are up early," Kiley says. Then, oddly, her face softens. "How's Will?"

The air leaves my lungs so quickly, it's like I've been punched. Jacob blinks, and I stammer, "He's . . . he's . . ."

I can't say it. I've never actually *said it*, and I can't say it now.

"Dead," Jacob says at last. "Will died. About a month ago."

Kiley was already pale, but she somehow gets even paler. Her hands start to tremble, and I'm super focused on that knife she's holding. Her face crumples.

"I knew he was sick, but I—I didn't . . ." Her voice catches.

"Do you . . . uh . . . happen to have Will's laptop charger?" I ask. But she's sobbing, almost too loudly, and she doesn't seem to hear me.

Or pretends not to?

Jacob glares at her, at the knife she's holding, studying her every move. He grabs my hand. "We're sorry to tell you. We, uh, better . . . go?"

"Wait!" Kiley screams. She dashes around the counter. The knife glistens in her grip. It sets my teeth on edge. "I need to talk to you!"

Jacob pushes me through the door, then follows, Kiley and her knife just behind us. We dash to his car. He turns the engine over—it starts right away, thank goodness—and slams the car into drive. Kiley races into the parking lot, knife gleaming. I can barely hear her over the squealing tires and grumbling engine: "Chloe! Will's charger! Wait!"

Jacob swings the car into a nearby gas station. The neon lights inside the store flicker, and the jumping shadows send a thrill down my spine. Jacob and I are both panting. "What the . . . ," he says, eyes wide. I shake my head.

And then, for some reason, we laugh. Like maniacal

idiots, we laugh. It's like those weird moments when you giggle at a funeral or chuckle in church—all our fear finds escape through laughter. We laugh until tears stream down our faces.

"She's faking it," Jacob says when he finally catches his breath. He knocks a fist against the steering wheel. "Uncle Will's obit was in the newspaper. We posted it on Facebook. How could she *not know*? Chloe, that is our number one suspect right there!"

I still can't really put words together. My stomach twists in a tight knot and my eyes sting *again*.

It's so weird, how it feels like Uncle Will dies all over again every time we tell someone he's gone.

It's so weird, being chased by someone with a knife.

Jacob hesitates. I can tell he wants to say something.

"What?" I ask. He's not one to hold back words.

He takes a deep breath. "Cyanide. I was curious about it since, you know, I'd never heard of it, and it was such a weird word for Charlie to know. So I googled it."

I blink and chuckle. "Hope you're not on some government watch list now."

He laughs a hollow laugh. Not what I was expecting. He's serious. "Yeah. Listen. I read about this guy in Chicago a few years ago. He won a million dollars in the lottery, but the very next month, he was dead. The police said it was natural causes, until one of the guy's relatives asked them to dig a little further. Turns out, he had eaten a lethal dose of cyanide. The police didn't even know to look for poison, see. Sometimes, cyanide poisoning can mimic all sorts of diseases. If the doctors don't know to test for it, they just assume . . ."

I'm nodding. My heart kicks it up a notch. "They assume it's a genetic disease. But it could've been poison."

Jacob shrugs. "So sayeth the internet."

He cranks the engine. Just before we swerve out onto the road, Jacob adjusts his rearview mirror and clears his throat. "Chloe, *don't turn around.*"

So of course I turn around. I peer out the back window. "What?"

Jacob hisses at me—hisses!—so I stiffly face forward again. "Listen. I don't want freak you out. But there's a yellow Prius behind us that's been following us since we left our block."

12

HE'S A SUSPECT!

A still life painting is a painting of things that are, well, still. It should be easy. The stuff is just *sitting there*. Ms. Umar says the painting is supposed to represent *us*, so I've grouped together a bunch of things I love on the coffee table in the living room: A *Howl's Moving Castle* DVD case. A Pokémon stuffie, Eevee. A Fanta can. A soccer ball. A coffee mug stuffed full of colored pencils.

But my painting is a bunch of blobs and shapes and messy colors instead of actual objects. It looks like the weird stuff you see swimming through goo when you look through a microscope. I huff and take a step back, squinting at the painting to see if it improves.

It doesn't improve.

I squeeze a dollop of yellow onto my palette. Adding yellow to another color is a bit like adding white, but better—it adds a creamier, sunnier undertone to the other hue. It's a harder-working white. Straight out of the tube, this yellow is the *exact* shade of the yellow Prius that followed us from Grounded early this morning. I swirl it around on my palette. "Who are you?" I whisper to the dollop of sunny paint. "What do you want?"

I shake my head. Am I really whispering to paint? Geez.

Charlie clicks and whistles a small song. She waddles across the tabletop and knocks over the mug, watching the colored pencils clatter and roll across the living room floor.

"Oh, oops!" she says. "Good girl. Pretty bird. Fold your napkin." She hops down to the floor and starts batting the pencils around. Friendly hisses, twitches her whiskers, and skulks under the couch.

Mom's phone rings in the kitchen, and I hear her answer it: "Hello?"

"Teresa Alvarez?" someone shouts on speakerphone.

"Speaking," Mom answers. I drop to my knees and start picking up pencils.

"This is George Jones. Not the country music singer. Will's old landlord."

I freeze when I hear Uncle Will's name.

"Oh, hello—" Mom begins.

"Yeah, listen," George interrupts. "You gotta come clean out Will's apartment, or I gotta charge you another month's rent."

Wait. Uncle Will's apartment hasn't been cleaned out yet? I guess I assumed they would just take care of that. Then I realize: *we* are *they*.

"Oh," Mom says. I can hear her pacing the kitchen floor. Charlie clicks her disapproval that I'm taking away her pretty pencils. I lay my finger over my lips. "Shhhhh, Charlie."

Charlie squawks back, "Shhhhh, Charlie. Quiet, girl. This won't hurt."

I blink—*won't hurt*? How does she know that phrase? I strain my ears to hear Mom's conversation.

"I didn't even think about that, cleaning out his things. I've been so busy settling his medical bills and . . ."

"Yeah, well, it's time to think about it," the landlord grumbles through the phone. What a rude guy! "I'm not a storage unit for your dead brother's crap." I swear I hear him laughing with another guy on the other end of the call.

The air feels like it was sucked out of the house. I sit up and bonk my head on the underside of the table. "Ow!"

Charlie echoes, "Ow!"

My eyes widen and I whisper, "Charlie! This guy—he's a suspect for sure!"

Charlie shuffles, flaps her wings, and screeches, "Suspect! He's a suspect!"

"Shhhhh!"

But Mom and George don't seem to hear us in the background. Mom's taking deep breaths, and her voice is low in her reply. "There is no need to talk to me like that. We will come over next weekend and clear out Will's things." Oh boy. Her mad voice. That guy has done it—he's made an enemy of my mother.

"Nope!" George shouts over the speakerphone. "It's the end of the month. You'll come tomorrow, or I send you a bill for May's rent."

I lean over and peek into the kitchen. Mom is biting her lip. She seems to be weighing how terrible it would be to give a whole month's worth of rent money to this awful guy so she doesn't have to face this task yet, versus us just sucking it up and cleaning out Uncle Will's stuff.

Practicality wins. "Fine. We'll be there tomorrow." Mom stabs at the phone with her pointer finger to hang up, then tosses it onto a dish towel. "Ugh!" she growls.

I've never seen her so angry. My heart twists.

Mom stomps into the living room and doesn't even say a word about the colored pencils everywhere.

". . . clean out Will's apartment . . ." she's muttering as she paces.

A thought pops into my brain, like a cartoon lightbulb appearing overhead. If I help her clean Uncle Will's apartment, I might find his laptop charger! Uncle Frank swears he doesn't have it, and ordering a new one doesn't really seem to be a priority for him. And I'm definitely not asking that knife-wielding Kiley about it again. I just knew I was going to have to spring for a new one. If I find it, I won't have to get a job as a fart-soaked manatee. Win-win.

"Mom," I say, crawling out from under the table. She startles like she hadn't seen I was under there. "Sorry. I'll come with you. I'll help clean out Will's apartment."

Mom cracks her knuckles, nods. "Okay. Yep. You . . ." She waves her hand over her head, like she's talking about all of us in the house. "You're all coming. Everyone is coming. Frank, too. I'll need all the help I can get to sort through Will's things."

This is it. We find the laptop charger . . . we find the killer.

13

ENEMIES IN VIRGINIA

"You two ride with Uncle Frank," Mom says, donning sunglasses. "Grammy and I will be there in a bit. C'mon, Mom." Uncle Frank has a big new SUV that can fit a bunch of stuff, and it's grumbling at the base of our driveway now. Mom and Grammy walk up the street to find her parked car.

"Shotgun," Jacob calls, and jumps in the front seat.

"Shotgun!" Charlie echoes from her perch on my arm. I love that her tiny harness lets me bring her so many places.

I lift Charlie higher. "You don't mind if Charlie comes, too?"

Uncle Frank looks pained, but says, "No, not at all."

Charlie and I climb into the back seat. Uncle Frank's car smells tangy-new, so much so that I can taste the newness. Jacob inhales deeply. "That new car smell," he sighs. "Nothing smells better." I don't know why people love new car smells so much. It smells like chemicals to me.

"This car is *sick*, Uncle F," Jacob says, running a fingertip over the huge screen in the dashboard.

Uncle Frank grins. "Thanks. I had to wait weeks to get the exact model I wanted."

Jacob inhales deeply again. "Worth the wait, dude."

I have a memory snapshot of Uncle Will bending the branch of a magnolia tree my way—on top of which sat a huge creamy-white bowl of a blossom, perched on shiny-slick green leaves. A honeybee rolled around inside, bathing in pollen. I didn't even need to bend toward the flower to smell it. *Nothing smells better than magnolia, Chlo. It smells like home.* I'll record that one later, for sure.

I open my journal, and on the page marked *Suspects!*, I add *Will's rude landlord, George Jones (not the country music singer).* Now there are three names on the list: Uncle Frank, Kiley the ex, and the landlord.

Uncle Frank catches my eye in the rearview mirror. "What's that?"

I slam the journal shut. "Nothing."

"It's her suspect list," Jacob says, drumming on the dashboard.

"Suspect," Charlie echoes. "He's a suspect."

Uncle Frank quirks an eyebrow at Charlie in the mirror. "That's an odd word for a bird to know."

My lips flatten and I try in vain to quirk an eyebrow, too. "It *is*, isn't it?"

Jacob slaps the back of his hand against Uncle Frank's arm. "We know who did it, by the way. Who killed Uncle Will. Chloe's not ready to close the investigation, but I am."

I scowl at Jacob from the back seat. He shouldn't be discussing this with another suspect!

"Really? Who did it?" Uncle Frank says casually.

"Kaley. Will's ex."

"Kiley," I say, rolling my eyes. "And we're not sure. But she's pretty suspicious."

Jacob tells Uncle Frank all about our adventure to Grounded. "I mean, she was talking all about murder! She chased us with a *knife*, dude. She definitely did it."

Uncle Frank's forehead creases. "Y'all be careful, okay? I don't know Kiley that well, but I don't think she'd do something like that."

Jacob shrugs and keeps knocking his knuckles against the dashboard. Charlie bobs her head along with the beat.

We ride in silence the rest of the way to Uncle Will's apartment. Uncle Frank finds a spot to parallel park his SUV, and he glares into his rearview mirror. "That car behind us—there's no way the tint on those windows is legal. Look how dark that windshield is—you can't even see the driver inside! Crazy yellow Prius."

Jacob and I twist to the rear window, both shouting, "Yellow Prius!" The same car that followed us to Grounded.

The smaller car zips around us, and Jacob points. "Virginia plates."

I tap my purple sparkle pen against my lips. "Hmmm. Uncle Frank—did Uncle Will have any enemies in Virginia?"

14

NUMBER 13

Uncle Will lives—*lived*—in a rickety old townhouse down by the wharf. The building is hundreds of years old, literally, and has been standing next to the ocean so long, she's coated in a fine layer of silty salt. *She*—Uncle Will called all boats and buildings and cars *she*. The building is painted pink, and it's crumbling, and the whole block smells like fish, but Uncle Will loved this place, loved watching the boats come and go as he sat dangling his legs off the rusty fire escape. "Mi casa," he'd say, taking the steps up to the third floor two at a time. "I love her."

I sneak aside and record those thoughts.

We trudge up the dark, narrow, creaky stairs.

Charlie seems to recognize the place; she cocks her head left, right, up, and starts flapping on my elbow. I hope to calm her; she doesn't need to try her terrible flying stunts here, three stories up.

The landlord, George Jones, stands in front of the apartment door, number 14. The moment he sees my mom, his mouth pulls into a knot.

"I'm so sorry about my tone yesterday, Mrs. Alvarez. The owner of this building—my boss, Mr. Grimmett? He was standing right next to me while I made the call. Mr. Grimmett don't tolerate no softness, you know? Real hardo, that guy. And I need this job. *Need*. Anyways, he's all bent up to rent this place out again." George the landlord sucks in a huge wavering breath. "Your brother. Will? That guy was one of a kind. He was the apple of everyone's heart!" George throws his arms around Mom's waist and sobs into her chest.

This George—he's a chameleon. Someone who changes who he is, depending on who he's with. I don't trust him.

George blubbers louder. His nose is snotty, and his hug has Mom's arms pinned to her ribs. She tries to pat his back but can only awkwardly fling her arms against her sides. Grammy chuckles, and Uncle Frank mashes his lips together to keep from laughing.

George finally breaks off the hug and swipes his

snotty nose on his sleeve. "Will was a good friend. A great tenant. Everybody here loved the guy," he says, motioning to the building. Of course they did. Will was awesome.

George takes out a huge key ring and unlocks the door with an actual old-school key. He stops before swinging it open. He peers over his weirdly tinted wire-rimmed glasses and snorts back his snot.

"Don't take the furniture. That's all mine. And listen. Don't tell the other tenants this, and definitely not Mr. Grimmett, but . . ." He looks over each shoulder, then stands on tiptoe to peer over us, apparently making sure no one else can hear this. His voice is a loud whisper. "I let a few months' rent slip when I heard Will was sick." He shakes his head, and his eyes get red again. "That guy was too young. Only the too-young die . . . young."

The knot in my throat returns. Also the knot in my stomach and the knot in my heart.

George swings the door wide, and sunlight floods the dark hallway. When he spins back to us, he introduces himself to Grammy and Uncle Frank: "George Jones. Not the country music singer." Then he blinks at me like he's just now seeing me. He smiles. "Hiya, Charlie! Welcome back, girl."

"AWK!" Charlie screeches. She flaps wildly, seeing

inside the apartment she once knew as home. "Charlie is a pretty girl! Pretty girl! AWK!"

The door behind us, number 13, swings wide. "HOLY LIVING COW IS THAT TERRIBLE BIRD BACK?"

A tiny man peeks out of apartment 13. He's bald on the top of his head but has long stringy shoulder-length hair growing down the sides. He wears stacks of wooden beads and a flowy shirt with flowers stitched on it. I'd expect someone with his hippie vibe to be chill, but he continues shouting.

"THAT BIRD IS THE WORST THING THAT EVER HAPPENED TO ME. I COULD MURDER WHOEVER BROUGHT THAT THING BACK!"

Uncle Frank side-eyes Mom, who gently pushes me and Jacob into Uncle Will's apartment. I hear Uncle Frank questioning the terrible neighbor, Number 13, as the door slides shut: "What do you mean, *murder* . . . ?"

I smile. Uncle Frank might still be a suspect, but he's also helping, just like he promised.

Charlie floats to the kitchen counter from her perch on my elbow. She struts and squawks and poops on the countertop like she owns the place. Which I guess she once did.

"Jacob, you take the living room," Mom says. "Mom, pack up the bathroom. Chloe, you take—"

"I'll take his office," I interrupt. I motion to the nook that houses a desk, a lamp, and piles of paper. That's likely where Uncle Will's laptop charger would be, right? Mom hands me an empty cardboard box.

Jacob has pulled out the stopper on a giant inflatable dachshund, the kind you bring to a swimming pool. He's rolling around on the living room floor with it, trying to squish the air out of it, *fweeeeeeeeee-wwwwweeeee.* Mom unplugs a string of white lights that decorates a healthy palm tree, also adorned with strands of purple, gold, and green Mardi Gras beads. Charlie struts back and forth on the kitchen counter, then pecks at one of the cabinet doors. I open it, and there's birdseed inside.

"Smart girl," I say, and pour her a dish. I turn to the office.

I unplug the lamp, wrap the cord around it, and put it in the box, along with the squashed pillow from his chair. I leaf through the stack of paper, mostly doctors' bills marked OVERDUE in bright red ink. I hold them up to show Mom. "What do I do with these?"

Mom squints at them, sighs. "Box them up, I guess. I suppose I should contact all those folks and let them know . . ."

She doesn't finish that sentence—*let them know Will died.*

I dump them in the box, along with the contents of

the desk drawer: Paper clips. Pens. Old headphones. A sticky note with the name *Deloris* and a phone number on it. A clue? I slide that one into my pocket. I'll find you, Deloris.

The office is done, and there's no laptop charger here.

I glance at Mom, standing at the edge of the kitchen, looking overwhelmed. I offer my elbow to Charlie, who hops on board.

"I'll start on his bedroom," I say. Mom inhales, bites her lip.

I give her a quick side-hug. "We got this, Mom. We're a team."

She clears her throat. "You're right. A team." Her eyes soften at me, and I feel the emotion behind her gaze: pity. "How're we doing, kiddo?" she asks.

My stomach roils. Do I tell her my theory?

"I know how much you miss him," she says. "I do, too."

Oh, that. Not the murder, but the *missing*. I swallow hard. "Yeah."

She cocks her head at me. She's waiting for a better answer.

I wiggle my dark phone screen toward her. "Dad's idea about recording all these memories of Will—it's really helping."

Mom runs a hand down the back of my hair. "Good.

I'm so glad you're doing that. Can I maybe . . . listen to them sometime? Or are they just for you?"

I shift. "Maybe? I haven't thought about anyone else listening to them." The thought makes me a little nauseous, honestly, but I don't say that.

Mom squeezes my hand. "You can talk to me, too, if you want. I know I'm not as impartial as a voice recorder, though." She chuckles oddly. I'm not sure what she means by that, but it's nice to hear. I smile at her, and she smiles back.

Mom opens the first kitchen drawer and digs in.

Charlie flaps her wings wildly when we enter Will's room. I immediately see why: she floats down to a table in the corner of the room, where there's a box of bright toys and mirrors and bells. She starts pulling items from the plastic bin and tossing them around the room, squawking and shouting. "Pretty bird! I love you, Charlie!"

"Did you find your toys, girl?" I say, and run a finger down her back.

Charlie ignores me. She's way too excited about her toys. She squeaks a rubber duckie, then imitates the squeak perfectly. She hasn't paced or plucked a single feather since she's been here. It's nice to see her so calm.

I strip the bed, pack up the dresser drawers and the closet. It's heavy and a lot of work. The *stuff* we leave behind when we . . . leave . . . is overwhelming. And Uncle Will didn't even prioritize this stuff. *People and experiences over things, Chlo-dog!* I can hear him saying as I pack up his World Series of Poker shirt. *Carpe diem!*

"Carpe diem," I mutter, and toss six decks of cards in the box.

"That bird is chewing on a cord," I hear from the doorway. I jump. I thought I was alone. I turn to the door.

It's the neighbor from across the hall, Number 13! I gulp. He's silhouetted in the doorframe, the light from the hallway masking his face in shadows. And he's holding—is that a sledgehammer?! My heart races, my stomach churns. I take a step back.

Number 13 raises the club slowly, slowly . . . I wince, squint my eyes. But he points to the corner table with his tool. It's not a sledgehammer. It's a spool of packing tape.

Jacob pushes past the neighbor and chuckles. "A cord? I find that shocking. Get it?! SHOCKING? HA!" Jacob laughs at his own joke. He hefts a box of clothing onto his hip and pushes out of the room.

Number 13 waves the packing tape at the corner again. "Listen, it's no skin off my back if that bird fries like a chicken. But you should probably stop that thing before *ZAP!*" Number 13 shouts and stomps his foot on the hardwood floor.

Charlie startles and squawks, flapping her wings at the neighbor. Number 13's face curls and he scurries backward. I turn to Charlie at last. In one of her long claws, she's gripping a thick black electrical cord.

Will's laptop charger!

I cram the laptop charger in my backpack and dance a little jig because I don't have to wear a stinky old manatee costume for money! I don't have to wait for Uncle Frank to decide to order it! I don't have to be chased by Will's exes and their knives! Hooray!

I offer my elbow to Charlie and head out of the room. Jacob and Uncle Frank have started competing to see who can lift the most boxes. That kind of horseplay around Charlie scares me; her bones are so delicate. I get nervous about that kind of stuff now.

In the living room, Number 13, who I hear is named Boris, is taping boxes shut with a loud *scruuuuuuuueeeeee* of the tape dispenser. Boring Boris. He's still talking to my mom about Charlie, apparently: "That bird is *awful*. I'm over there trying to meditate—trying to CALM MY NERVES!—and that bird's over here all '*Caw! Caw!*'"

Charlie lifts her beak and echoes him, "Caw! Caw!"

It makes me laugh, because it sounds more like a bird saying *Caw! Caw!* than it does a bird actually cawing.

Boring Boris looks up from the box he's taping and scowls. "That bird is a mess! So smelly! Dander and feathers and poop everywhere!"

This man is singing Mom's song. She's nodding along with his every complaint, muttering *mmmhmm* under her breath.

"And so LOUD!" Boris shouts unironically. "SO LOUD! I could wring that bird's neck, if I wasn't so calm from all my meditating."

Mom's eyes shoot wide open. "What?"

Charlie must get a sense of the room, because she cocks her head and busts out with: "Homicide! Homicide! It was murder!"

Mom shifts her focus to Charlie, but the confused look on her face remains. Boris goes completely white.

"I don't know what your brother was teaching that horrible bird," he mutters. He returns to taping a box: *scruuuuuuuueeeeee*.

Number 13, Boris the Not-So-Boring, is getting added to the suspects list for sure.

15

YOU CAN'T HIDE

Mom is almost done packing up Uncle Will's kitchen, and she eyes the small plastic box tucked into a corner on the counter. "Still had an answering machine," she mutters with a weak smile. She pushes the flashing red button.

Uncle Will's voice sings through the small speakers: *"Hi, you've reached Will! If you're part of the problem, just hang up. If you're part of the solution, leave a message!"*

His voice! My throat closes, hearing him so chipper.

Mom's weak smile grows stronger. Charlie squawks and flaps and poops at hearing Uncle Will's voice.

Then, the messages:

Will, this is Dr. Rashaad. You missed your appointment again. We'd really love to follow up with you. Give us a call, okay?

This is a representative of the Low Country Collection Agency, reaching out to Will Calhoun again. We need you to call us immediately.

Hello! This is an automated message from Walgreens Pharmacy, calling to let you know we will hold your medications for five more days. Please come pick them up. Thank you.

There are a few more depressing messages like that. My heart sinks lower. Mom's smile has disappeared.

And then a gruff voice shouts through the small speakers: "*Will! Your cell voice mail is full, and Snooker gave me this number. I told you I could always find you, Will. You can't hide. Did you think you could hide? Pay up by the first of the month or you're done. Done!*"

The phone clicks and a loud, dull dial tone buzzes throughout the apartment. I look around. Mom, Boring Boris, Uncle Frank, Grammy, Jacob, and George the landlord stand there stunned, eyeing one another.

Charlie clicks, whistles, and sails off my arm to the

back of the couch. She flaps her wide wings. "You can't hide! *Squawk!* Can't hide! Pretty girl!"

Jacob shoulders the last of the boxes and heads out of the apartment. Mom takes Grammy's elbow and guides her behind him. I scan the apartment for clues one last time. Uncle Frank and George the landlord huddle together in the hall.

Two suspects whispering? I mean, Uncle Frank is close to being marked off the list—he was telling the truth about the charger, after all—but *I* decide when someone is no longer a suspect. My investigation, my suspects list. I inch closer, Charlie perched on my shoulder.

Uncle Frank rips a check out of his checkbook. "This should cover the three months' rent Will missed. Thank you for being so kind to my brother."

George nods, takes the check, and puts it in his shirt pocket. "I'm as grateful as a fiddle, Frank. Thanks." Old George just can't get a metaphor right, it seems.

Uncle Frank pauses. "And, um . . . do you know anything about that message?" He doesn't have to clarify which one.

George looks over his shoulder, which is weird, because he's in a corner in a dark hallway. He leans toward Uncle Frank. "Listen. Will owed a lot of people money. But that? That was definitely Jaws."

Charlie stops pecking at my hair and shouts, "Jaws! *Awk!*"

"Shhhhh!" I hush her. She returns to pecking a strand of my hair.

"Jaws?" Uncle Frank asks. He cracks his knuckles, his tell for when he's nervous.

"Yeah. I . . . uh . . . sorry to tell you this, but your brother owed a lot of money to some guy named Jaws. I was scared for Will, you know? I really thought Jaws might come after him."

My heart pounds in my ears. Charlie clicks twice and repeats, "Jaws! Jaws!"

Uncle Frank is now beet red, and the temper we saw at the lawyer's office is boiling under his skin. "Do you know where we can find this . . . *Jaws?*"

George is shaking his head before Uncle Frank even finishes asking the question. "No. Oh, no. You're barking up the wrong flagpole there, fella. Don't you go looking for Jaws, you hear? That guy finds out your brother died while still owing money, he comes after *you.* CHOMP!" At that, George throws his arms out and claps them together, acting out a huge shark bite.

Uncle Frank knocks his knuckles against the drywall. Walks toward me.

I slide backward toward the living room and try to look like I heard none of that. I pretend to study the fabric on an armchair while Charlie whistles like we are totally innocent. Uncle Frank eyes us.

"Chloe," he says, his voice wavering. "I'm all in." His jaw is tight and his eyes are red and watery, but hard. I gulp.

All in. That's poker terminology. It means he's putting all his chips into the game.

It means he believes me that Uncle Will was murdered.

On the ride home, Jacob takes a small wad of paper from his pocket. "Guys, look what I found in a pair of Uncle Will's cargo shorts." He smooths the rectangle of paper out on Uncle Frank's dashboard.

"A check?" Uncle Frank's eyes dart from the road to the check and back.

"Made out to Uncle Will," Jacob says, tapping it. "From Kiley. For $1,500."

Uncle Frank whistles. "That's not chump change." I don't know what he means by that, but $1,500 is a lot of money.

At a stoplight, Uncle Frank says, "Can I see that?" He examines the check, front and back. "Will never endorsed it." He points to the back of the check. It's blank.

Jacob shrugs. "What does that mean?"

The light turns green, and Uncle Frank hands the check to me in the back seat. It's been crumpled so much, the paper is soft and worn, like cloth.

"He never cashed it. She wrote him this check, but he wouldn't take the money."

Jacob pulls a face. "Why would someone do that? NOT take $1,500?"

Uncle Frank raises an eyebrow and looks in the rearview mirror at me. "If Will thought the money was dirty, maybe?"

"Dirty money?" I think back to Grammy's podcasts. "Like, money from illegal things?"

Jacob knocks his knuckles on the dashboard. "Dirty money. Huh. This Kiley is up to no good, I tell ya."

I run my fingertip over Kiley's signature: *Kiley Albertson*. Kiley Albertson, Crime Lord.

"What's this little heart over here?" I hold the check so Uncle Frank can see it in the mirror and point to the lower left corner of the check.

Uncle Frank looks. "That's the notes section. Most people use that to write what the check is for. You know, like 'April Rent' or 'Babysitter.' That kind of thing."

Kiley drew a heart on her dirty money? That is just stone cold, right there. Or a threat.

I think about this on the rest of the drive home: If Uncle Frank, an ACTUAL ADULT WHO IS

EXCELLENT AT ADULTING, believes that Will's death could've been foul play, it *really could've been* foul play. The hairs on the back of my neck prickle. Deep fear feels cold to the core. I need to really consider what it would mean to expose Kiley or George or Boris or the mysterious caller named Jaws as a killer.

16

FIVE SUSPECTS NOW

Mom's been using Will's laptop as a doorstop to hold our old wonky pantry door closed. When we get home, I pick it up off the kitchen floor, and the pantry door swings open. The universe is telling me I need Cheetos. Charlie, who is still on my shoulder, squawks when she sees the bag. She *loves* Cheetos. She leaves a little orange party behind every time she eats them. Literally behind. Who knew bird poop could be orange?

I bring Uncle Will's laptop to my room and plug it in. I don't want Mom to see it here, so I cover it with a few sheets of paper and a folded-open Powerpuff Girls comic book. Not suspicious at all.

While it's charging, Charlie and I munch on Cheetos and help the others move the boxes from Uncle Frank's car into the house. Mom leaves to gather another box, and Uncle Frank hisses to the rest of us, "Gang! Huddle!"

I smirk. "You've really got to update your mystery slang, Uncle Frank. The Scooby-Doo stuff is retro and all, but you could use something fresh."

Uncle Frank dismisses me with a wave of his hand. His face—he's serious.

"Chloe, I really think you're onto something with this murder business," he whispers. "I mean, *Jaws*?"

Grammy frowns, shakes her head. "Don't encourage her, Frank."

"Mom!" Uncle Frank whisper-hisses. "Think about how fast Will died. Couldn't it have been . . . poison?"

Goose bumps run down my arms. Jacob leans out of our huddle and whistles, long and low.

Grammy licks her teeth. Shakes her head again. "I can't be a part of this." She heads outside to help Mom. I note that she doesn't say, *No, Frank, there's no way it could've been poison*.

Uncle Frank lifts his chin at my backpack, sitting on a kitchen barstool. "Your list of suspects, Chloe. Can you read them to me?"

I fish out the spiral notebook. It's tattered, what

with all the pecking and nibbling Charlie has done on it while I've stared holes in the page labeled *Suspects!*

"Okay," I say and clear my throat, because there at the top of the list . . .

"Well, um, you, Uncle Frank." I burn, embarrassed, but I shrug. "Sorry."

But oddly, instead of working up his temper more, this seems to calm him. He suppresses a grin. "I understand. Smart to keep me on there until you're sure."

I smile and nod at the page. "Okay. Then there's Kiley the ex—"

"She still gets my vote," Jacob says, snapping his fingers. "She seems so . . . *murder-y.*"

I roll my eyes. "George the Landlord and Boring Boris from apartment 13. They were both . . . rude."

As I say it, I realize that *rude* and *murderer* are far apart when it comes to personality flaws, but no one else points that out, so they stay on the list.

Uncle Frank fishes in his pocket and produces a slim, shiny gold pen. One of the fancy ones. He offers it to me.

"Add Jaws."

I add the name Jaws. Even the word—*Jaws*—looks stabby and pointy. Like teeth. I shiver. "That's five suspects now."

Uncle Frank and Jacob huddle over the list. Uncle

Frank sucks in a huge breath, cracks his knuckles. "We're really onto something here, Chlo. I do think . . . I think it was murder."

Charlie drops her Cheeto nubbin and shivers her feathers from beak to tail tip. "Skull! Skull! It was murder! Alexa, play Def Leppard!"

"Pour Some Sugar on Me" blasts from our Alexa, and I shake Cheeto crumbs out of my hair while Uncle Frank and Jacob stare holes through the list of suspects.

Uncle Frank really does believe me!

Before bed, I sit at my desk. The laptop is finally charged. Charlie has climbed onto my pillow, chasing a hissing Friendly away. She mutters something that sounds like "No elbows on the table!" and throws a wing over her head. She settles in with a rustle. "Don't poop there," I warn her. She clicks twice, like she understands. *Click-click. Okay.*

I flip open the laptop. Dang. It's password protected. THIS is where Uncle Will suddenly becomes an adult?

I start with an obvious try: *carpe diem*. Nope.

I try *seize the day*. Nada.

I type in the *Robin Hood* song, *Oo-De-Lally*. And not only is that a no, but a window pops up that reads, *Access blocked due to too many sign-in attempts. You may try again in 24 hours.*

I slam the laptop shut. Only three password attempts per day? Uncle Will is suddenly a double adult?!

I lean back in my chair and think. Three attempts per day! It will take forever to get into this laptop. Meanwhile, Uncle Will's murderer roams free.

All my options seem to lead to more questions. I decide to call the number on the Post-it note I found in Uncle Will's apartment. Deloris. It rings four times. Five. I'm about to hang up when the voice mail picks up. The voice is deep and froggy:

"Hello. You've reached Madam Deloris, renowned psychic and medium. I can't come to the phone right now because I'm out here saving the world, one reading at a time. Leave a message. Or don't. It's your future we're talking about, hon." Beeeeeeeep.

I hang up.

A psychic? Why in the world would Will be talking to a psychic?

17

WE NEED TO FOLLOW HER!

Before I fall asleep, I place a $1,500 check that was never cashed and a Post-it note with a psychic's phone number on it in my purple spiral notebook, and I place *that* under my pillow.

"Okay, subconscious, get to work," I say aloud, punching the pillow. "Brain, let's dream about a killer." I don't think this'll work, honestly, but I'm getting desperate.

I sleep super soundly, no dreams at all, but I wake up to an earthquake. No, not an earthquake, I realize, my eyes peeling open. Jacob, jumping on my bed.

"Happy Saturday, Squeak. Get up," he says, bouncing. "I want to do a campout across from Grounded today. Keep an eye on Kaley. Ask her about that check."

"Stakeout. Kiley," I grumble.

"Uncle Frank is picking us up. He made me promise we wouldn't do anything without him."

I sit up slowly. "Okay."

Jacob does this fake pro wrestling move where he flings himself at me and it looks like he's going to slam his elbow down on my head. He doesn't, of course, but I wince anyway and punch him on the shoulder.

"Grammy wants to come, too. I don't think she believes us, but she's too curious to miss out. That woman has major FOMO."

I grin sleepily. Believes *us*, he said. We're suddenly a team of detectives. "All right. Give me five minutes."

Jacob squints and grins, too. "You know what? I'm proud of you, Squeak. You're listening to your gut here. Coach always says our gut is smarter than our heart and our head combined. Uncle Will . . ." He pauses for a second and gulps hard. "He'd be real proud of you."

Not Jacob getting all mushy first thing on a Saturday morning? I blink back sting and smile.

Jacob springs off my bed and lands on the wood floor with a thud. "And brush those teeth, Squeak. *Dang*, you're kicking some serious morning breath."

I dragon-breathe after him, tongue out,

hhhhhhaaaaaaaa. But I'm not even ticked. Jacob believes me, too. My family—they're going to help me solve Uncle Will's murder!

Uncle Frank eyes Charlie, perched on my shoulder, as we duck into his car. "Don't worry. I brought the baby wipes," I say, climbing into the back seat. I've learned to bring baby wipes everywhere I go with Charlie. This bird craps every ten minutes, I think.

We haven't driven a block before Jacob loud-whispers, "Y'all. The yellow Prius. It's back." He's sitting stiffly, like he's scared to make any sudden movements.

I don't know why he's whispering. It's not like the Prius can hear us.

Grammy and I both turn to check out the car. Charlie cocks her head like she's trying to see, too.

"It looks like Teresa's car," Grammy says, squinting through the morning glare on the back window.

Jacob nods. "That's why I first noticed it. But it's yellow. Mom's car is white. The windows are tinted darker, too. And this car has Virginia plates."

"Virginia . . . ?" Grammy says. She faces forward again. Licks her teeth.

The windows of the car following us are dark, mirrored. You can't see inside. Anyone could be lurking in that darkness. I shiver.

We get to Grounded and Uncle Frank swings hard into the gravel lot across from the shop. Rocks spew everywhere. The Prius swerves around us and zips right by.

We all exhale. Uncle Frank swipes a hand down his face. "What are we getting ourselves into?"

We're bored. We sit in Uncle Frank's new-smelling car with the AC blasting. Grammy runs her fingers over the tight stitches of her leather seat. "This is a gorgeous car, Frankie. I'm so proud of you and your success."

Uncle Frank blushes. I guess you never get past that, wanting to make your parents proud.

Charlie entertains us for the next hour with phrases like *hot stuff* and *peekaboo* and *dessert fork* and *crime scene*. Jacob watches Kiley first, then Grammy.

"This feels icky," Grammy says, lowering the binoculars. She unbuckles her seat belt. "I'm going to pee."

"NO!" we shout in unison. Jacob adds, "You can't go into Grounded! She'll recognize you. She knew me and Chloe right away."

Grammy smirks and points to the smoothie shop next door to Grounded. "What, do you think I'm a dumbbutt?"

Grammy hops out of the car, whistling, and swings her purse in a circle as she ducks into the Smoothie

Palace. Very subtle, Gram.

We sit. We wait some more. Charlie says, "Alexa, play the Eagles." Uncle Frank pulls up an Eagles playlist in his car for her. We have a car dance party.

But man, this is still so boring.

Uncle Frank huffs a deep sigh and looks in his rearview mirror. "I wonder what's taking Mom so long?"

We sit another minute in silence. "I'm going to go check on her," he says, and hops out of the car, too.

The moment the door to Smoothie Palace closes behind Uncle Frank, Kiley exits Grounded. She stalks down the street, obviously in a hurry.

"There she is!" Jacob whispers, and we duck. "We need to follow her! Where are Uncle Frank and Gram?"

I peel Charlie off my arm and hand her to Jacob. "I'll follow her. You start the car and pull in front of Smoothie Palace."

"I don't know . . . ," Jacob says. But we're already scrambling out of the car. He glances up the street at Kiley, now a block away. "Be careful, Squeak."

"I will," I say. I dash down King Street after her blue hair. She's fast, and I'm trying to stay far enough behind her so I can't be seen, but close enough not to lose her. Luckily, that hair makes her easy to track.

Kiley turns left, crossing Morrison Drive onto Algonquin Road. It feels like she's leading me out of the way or something; you couldn't take this path in a car. The trees are taller here. Shadows help. I duck from dark patch to dark patch. I feel like a villain. It's both thrilling and totally creeping me out, how easy it is to fall into this role.

My phone rings.

"Hello?" I whisper as Kiley turns right onto Huguenin Avenue. I've never been in this part of Charleston before. The buildings are older, tighter. Warehouses, with no windows. They look like places filled with giant spiderwebs and saws and unidentified stains on the floor.

"Chloe, where are you?" Uncle Frank shouts over the phone.

I look at the cross street. "Huguenin and Prosper," I whisper. "Don't worry, I can still see her."

"I'm not worried about her. I'm worried about *you*!" he shouts.

Grammy says, "Tell her she's being a dumbbutt." Grammy doesn't realize Uncle Frank is on speakerphone and I can hear her every word. "Tell her to stay right where she is!"

Jacob adds, "Drop us a pin, Chlo! We'll get to you!"

Almost as if Kiley can hear the shouting through my phone, she whips around. I hang up on Uncle Frank and leap sideways, into a dark doorway, and wait.

I peek around the corner. No Kiley!

I dash up the street, peering in every store. She's not in the check-cashing place. Not in the pawn shop. Not in the vape store. Finally, I spot her at the end of a long, dark alley. I move as fast as I can on tiptoe, avoiding trash spilling out of dumpsters and puddles of stuff that doesn't smell like rainwater. Something hisses at me, and I jump.

Kiley turns left out of the alley. I follow. Did the sun duck behind the clouds? Why does it suddenly feel colder, darker?

Kiley stops at last, next to a large wrought-iron gate that looks like twists of charred bones. She touches the gate with such tender reverence, I lose all my fear and my heart wrenches for her instead. Then she steps through the gate.

"Oh no," I breathe. "Not here, Kiley."

My phone pings with a text from Jacob: **where r u**

I send him a pin. I can't believe I'm sending them this location:

Magnolia Cemetery.

18

THE OBVIOUS ANSWER IS GHOSTS

Magnolia Cemetery has trees older than America's been a country, and the branches hang heavy and low, like reaching, grabbing arms. Spanish moss dangles from the limbs, looking like huge tangles of spiderweb. Traps. The headstones are colossal and ancient, some crumbling, the etchings long faded, making it impossible to read whose bones lie below. There are mausoleums, people buried aboveground in small, cold, marble cases, thanks to Charleston being the target of many a hurricane. Bodies have been known to wash away if you're not buried properly here. You can *feel* the spirits in this cemetery, unsettled, moaning alongside the massive, swaying tree branches.

I shudder.

Kiley weaves her way between headstones and disappears into shadows behind the pyramid mausoleum. It's famous—it's been in a lot of movies and photos. The day is now twilight, getting dark. I take note of Kiley's direction and wait for the others. *No way* am I following her into a graveyard solo.

Uncle Frank, Jacob, Charlie, and Grammy tumble in about three minutes later. Grammy and Uncle Frank run up to me, pat me, inspect me, almost like they're checking to make sure I'm still in one piece.

"Don't ever do that again, child," Grammy says, squeezing me to her chest. She smells like too much perfume covering cigarette smoke. "You scared the daylights out of me."

Jacob hands Charlie to me and bounces on his toes. He whistles long and low. "Get a load of this! Can you think of a better place for a murderer to hang out?"

We all scan the cemetery and collectively shiver.

"She went that way," I say, and point toward a grave marker of a stone baby lying in a stone carriage. It's life-size and creepy as all get-out. We follow the path.

After only a few steps, Uncle Frank stops short. "Shhh!" he whispers. "Do you hear something?" Sure enough, it sounds like Kiley is talking to someone. Lots of someones. And they're *talking back*.

Chills chase down my spine and my eyes widen. "Who is she talking to?" I whisper back. "In a *cemetery*?" The obvious answer is ghosts.

My heart races. Charlie shivers like hers is racing, too.

Jacob lays a finger over his lips, then motions for us to follow.

We tiptoe closer, closer . . .

"*Awk!*" Charlie screams. "Cowabunga! God save the Queen! Alexa, play Prince! *Awk! Click-click!*"

I die. Or at least, I panic so much, it feels like my soul leaves my body.

Kiley peers around a headstone that looks like a mini Washington Monument. She blinks in the now purple light. "Charlie? Chloe? Jacob? Are you guys . . . *following* me?"

"No!" Jacob, Uncle Frank, and I all say too loudly. We shake our heads and stumble through our denials.

"No!"

"Of course not!"

"Nuh-uh."

Grammy steps forward, tugs at the hem of her blazer, and clears her throat. "Yes, dear, we are. These three think you killed my son."

Okay, so if I thought I died a moment ago, I was wrong. I'm dying *now*, in the silence that follows that statement. Leave it to Grammy.

Jacob gulps. Uncle Frank stares at the ground so hard, I think it might catch fire. I shift under the weight of Charlie on my shoulder and bite my lip.

Kiley's eyes widen.

And then she tosses her head back and lets loose the deepest, heartiest laugh.

We all eye each other. And then we all laugh, too. It feels great, laughter after fear. A big release.

"Whew," Kiley sighs at last. "Well, join the tour, I guess."

"Tour?" Uncle Frank asks.

We look past Kiley, and at last we see it: a whole crowd of folks, watching our conversation. They appear to be alive and well and very interested in our murderous accusations.

"The tour?" Kiley says. "The Charleston Historical Ghost Tour. Join us!"

19

THE HISTORICAL GHOST TOUR

Kiley weaves down the narrow pea-gravel path between the ancient, crumbling headstones, shining her weak flashlight on a few.

"Here lies Lavinia Fisher," Kiley whispers, her voice a creepy croon. The headstone reads *Lavinia Fisher, 1793–1820.* "Lavinia became famous as America's first female serial killer."

I shiver. Jacob's eyes widen and he whacks Uncle Frank's arm. "What?"

"Lavinia and her husband owned the Six Mile Wayfarer House, which was an inn for weary travelers. These tired souls would be fed, and Lavinia would pound them with questions over dinner, seeking to learn if they had money or valuables of any sort. If they did, Lavinia would poison their tea. When the travelers were sound asleep from the haze of the poison, Lavinia would—BOOM!"

Here Kiley shouts and claps, and everyone—every last one of us—jumps. Including Charlie, who flusters her feathers on my shoulder.

"She would pull a lever and the bed would collapse. The victims would drop into a deep pit, *never to be heard from again.*"

Grammy nods. "Well, that's one way to get rid of houseguests," she whispers. Uncle Frank holds in a chuckle. Kiley appears to be suppressing a smile, too.

"Lavinia was sentenced to death for her crimes. Hanged in Charleston's town square."

Hanged. That's the word Kiley used on the phone the day Jacob and I overheard her conversation at Grounded. I remember because it sounded so weird; I thought the right word would be *hung*.

Charlie cocks her head at the word *Charleston*. "Pretty bird," she murmurs softly. Even she seems to know this place requires quiet. She whistles a soft two-note ditty.

"And here!" Kiley whips her flashlight beam around, and the effect is dizzying. "Beneath this soil lie the bones of James McAfee, who many believe to be the Gray Man ghost. Legend has it that two hundred years ago, James was riding on horseback to check on his fiancée during a horrific storm, when a tree fell and killed him. Many believe that his ghost still haunts the South Carolina coast, showing up to warn us of coming storms."

The Gray Man. Kiley talked about him on that phone call, too. Charlie shifts on my shoulder and I jump, imagining a ghost placing his cold, gray hand there. . . .

"And here!" Kiley's cyclone of a flashlight beam lands on a small, simple headstone carved only with the name Alice. Something about the simplicity of the headstone looks painful. "Here lies Alice Flagg. Alice was born into a very wealthy South Carolina family, and she fell in love with a lumberjack. Her family forbid her to marry him, saying he was 'below her station.' She accepted an engagement ring from him and wore it secretly around her neck, strung on a ribbon. When her mother discovered that Alice was engaged, she forced Alice to give the ring back and sent her to school far away from Charleston. Alice couldn't eat, couldn't sleep, so intense was the depth of her lost love. She fell into a coma and wasted away, her heart broken."

Here Kiley pauses. She swallows past a lump in her throat, almost like she knows the taste of heartbreak herself.

From Uncle Will?

Kiley inhales deeply and continues: "There are

many stories of young ladies standing over this very grave, Alice's grave, and having their wedding rings fly off their fingers. Their rings are lost forever in the tall, marshy grass."

Fell into a coma. That was in Kiley's phone call, too. It made me a little sick at the time. It sounded so much like what happened to Uncle Will. . . .

All those things she said on the phone: They weren't her plans, or a recap of her wrongdoings. They were part of this ghost tour.

The relief I feel is like peeling off wet socks after a long, sweaty soccer match.

Kiley isn't our killer.

After the tour, Kiley approaches us. She's blinking fast, and her jaw shifts. "I'm so sorry about Will," she says, her voice wavering. She's looking specifically at Grammy. "I cared about him a lot. I wish he hadn't closed himself off from everyone there at the . . . end."

He had shut her out, too? Who did he have in his life when he was getting sicker and sicker?

Kiley clears her throat, keeps going: "Things were getting serious, or so I thought. And then at the beginning of the year, he just pulled back. Closed himself off. Stopped calling and texting. It happened so fast. It was all so . . . surprising."

Uncle Frank, Jacob, and I all nod like an army of

bobbleheads. "Exactly!" I say. "He did the same to us. Weird, right?"

But Jacob isn't about to let his number one suspect off so easily. "Why did you give Will $1,500?"

Grammy licks her teeth. She does not like talking about money.

Kiley looks surprised, but not guilty. "Before he started backing away, he said something about his mounting bills. I didn't know they were medical bills, or I . . . I would've done more." Her eyes glass over again. "He refused to cash it, though. I'm surprised you found it. I would've thought he'd torn it up."

I know why he didn't tear it up. That little heart she drew in the notes section. It meant something to Uncle Will.

Uncle Frank seems to be thinking the same thing. He smiles at me, grabs my hand, and gives it a squeeze. He turns to Kiley. "This is a bit of an intense question, but did Will have any enemies? People that—"

"Oh, yeah," Kiley interrupts. "That guy who lives across the hall from him."

My lips flatten. "Boring Boris in number 13."

Kiley nods. "Boris. That's it. That guy *hated* Will. Or more specifically, Charlie. Boris and Will were friends until Charlie came along."

We all look at the silvery-gray bird on my shoulder. Charlie must feel the spotlight shift onto her, because she preens and crows, "Charlie is a pretty girl."

Kiley smiles a thin smile, like it's painful to tell us this next stuff. "That guy tried to get Will kicked out of his apartment. He called the cops when he thought Charlie was making too much noise. He even tried to break into Will's apartment once when Will was gone. Who knows what that weirdo was up to?"

"He broke into Will's apartment?" Grammy asks.

Jacob shifts his weight from foot to foot. "Boring Boris . . . ," he mutters, and cracks his knuckles. Grammy licks her teeth, loud.

Kiley reaches over and gently scratches Charlie's head. "Who would want to hurt a bird like this, huh?"

The back of my neck prickles. "A murderer. That's who."

That night, I scratch both Kiley the ex and Uncle Frank off the suspects list. The relief I feel is immediate, like a big, whooshing exhale. I don't have a whole lot of proof that they're both innocent, other than my heart telling me they are. My brain argues this, saying that a more prudent detective would mark no one off the list until the killer is found. The heart and the head argue a lot in an investigation like this one. Which is interesting, because I've noticed that the heart and the head argue a lot about grief, too.

20

PURE IMITATION

On the bus the next day, Audrey holds her phone to her forehead while I try to get her to guess the word on the screen. Audrey doesn't like to waste a minute of time; if our morning commute can be used to play Heads Up, then we'll play Heads Up.

The word is *camel*. "Uh, they can go a long time without drinking water?" I say.

"Snake!" Audrey guesses.

I giggle. "A snake can go a long time without *eating*."

She motions with her hand, *yeah, yeah, more clues*.

"It has a hump."

"Camel!"

"Yes!"

Audrey tilts the phone up. *Blink!* says the game. Correct.

The next word is *rhino*.

I make a horn motion off my nose. "It has . . . uh . . . one of these."

"Elephant!"

"No, a horn."

"Rhino!"

"Yep."

Tilt. *Blink!* Correct.

I grin like half a pie at the next word. "It's what Charlie is!"

"A bird!"

"What kind of bird?"

"A parakeet?"

"No, no. Bigger than a parakeet."

"Chloe, are you kidding? I have no idea. I've never even met the bird."

"You haven't? Huh . . ."

Audrey turns the phone around to read the word. "Parrot. Cool. Why haven't I met this bird yet?"

How do you tell your best friend that you've been spending all your time investigating your uncle's murder with your family, without her thinking you've all lost it?

You don't.

"I could come over after practice tonight!" she says.

"I want to meet this famous bird."

"No! I mean, uh . . . I can't . . ." I have to try to break into Will's laptop again tonight. Look over the suspects list. Do Google searches on Boring Boris. Figure out who Jaws is. Convince Jacob or Grammy to help me look for clues.

Audrey eyes me as I try to come up with something. I can't lie, but I definitely can't tell her the truth. I must take too long, because Audrey's face shadows over.

"Something's up with you lately, Chlo," Audrey says to her hands, folded in her lap. "You don't stick around after practice, and you bailed on the team when we went to see *Spider-Man*. *Spider-Man*! You're getting After School Detention—"

"Ahem! After School *Service*, thank you!"

"Fine. After School Service, and you're getting your phone taken up, in *art class*, and . . . well . . . are you mad at us? At *me*?"

"No!" I toss my arms around her shoulders and give her an awkward sideways bumpy-bus hug. "No. My family . . . we've had a rough patch since my uncle . . ."

My throat shuts. No more words.

Audrey squeezes my arm between her cheek and her shoulder, a mini hug. "Okay. I get that. When my grandma died, I was a mess."

I inhale sharply. Instead of feeling relief that Audrey

understands, I feel a twinge of anger. No, it's not the same! Uncle Will was young! Uncle Will was perfect! Uncle Will was *hurt by someone*! She can't possibly miss her grandma like I miss Will.

No. I shake my head to clear away that thought. I don't want to think cruel things like that. Of course she misses her grandma like I miss Uncle Will. Why is my brain so mean lately?

Audrey blinks, like she hears my thoughts. Sometimes I think she does. Good friends can hear the stuff that isn't said as clearly as the stuff that is. She pulls out of my hug. "If you ever want to talk about him, I'm here." It's quiet, the way she says this, and I can hear the tears underneath her voice.

I need to change this conversation, pronto. I clear my throat.

"Maybe Mom can bring Charlie to our next practice?" I know full well my mom isn't bringing that bird *any*where *any*time soon. "Not tonight, but the one after?"

Audrey's face brightens immediately, and she bounces on the green plastic bus seat. "Yes! She can be our mascot! Ooo, I wonder if they make tiny bird jerseys!"

I picture Charlie on the sidelines of the soccer field, squawking, "Skull! Skull! It was murder!"

"Yeah, okay," I mutter. My stomach churns. "Mascot."

Our still life paintings hang on Ms. Umar's pegboard wall. They have our grades penciled on the back. I got an A.

How does a crummy painting like mine still get an A? After class, I bring my still life up to Ms. Umar and ask, "So does everyone who turns in work get an A or what?"

She chuckles. "Do you not deserve a good grade, Chloe? I can certainly lower it if you want me to."

"No, no, I . . ." I try to figure out what I want to say. "I just—how did I get an A?"

Ms. Umar's brilliant smile softens. She runs her fingertips lightly over my painting. "Chloe, I can tell you picked items for your painting that mean a lot to you. You've arranged them in a very pleasing way. You've got shadows and light, depth and texture—it's a good piece."

My forehead crinkles and I sigh. It's not good enough. It's not a standout. It doesn't make me happy. But I nod.

"Chloe, friend," Ms. Umar says gently. She returns the painting to the pegboard, the wall she calls our "gallery," and gestures to all the paintings hanging there. "Everyone sees the world differently. Who am I to judge your perspective? Your vision? All I can truly do is grade your technique."

I can't believe what I'm about to say, but I know Ms. Umar will understand. "It just doesn't feel *important*, you know? I've . . ." I swallow. "I've been thinking a lot lately about what's important."

Ms. Umar feigns shock, her eyes wide, her fingers splayed across her chest, and gasps. I chuckle. "Not important? Not important, she says! Chloe, an artist named Jacques Lipchitz once said, 'Art is an action against death. It is a denial of death.' Art is so important! I truly believe that for some of us, it is why we are on this earth! To create! To share! To love! And to do so indefinitely!"

She is so enthusiastic, so passionate, I can't help but nod. I would really love to deny death right about now.

I look at my still life painting, mounted on the paint-splattered brown wall. It's okay, I guess. But if I didn't already know what those objects in the painting were, I wouldn't recognize them.

I wish I could paint like Charlie talks: pure imitation. She just straight-up copies sounds. There's no real meaning for her, as far as I can tell. If I could paint like that?

How happy I'd be if I could just neatly copy the world into a perfect, tidy painting.

21

Charlie splashes around in a shallow dish of water, taking a bath. She dunks her head, then dips each wing like she's washing her armpits. Wingpits? She shivers, cleaning around and under every feather. Precise. I had to coax her into the bath by floating small chunks of apple in the water, but now that she's in, she's having a blast.

"*Click-click!*" she says, and whistles a tune. She shakes like a dog and splatters water across my desk. I laugh.

I look back at the notebook. The suspects list. So many suspects, still. So frustrating. If only I could figure out Uncle Will's password. . . .

I inhale, crack my knuckles, crack my neck, like I

imagine hackers do before, I dunno, hacking into the Pentagon or something.

The first password I try: *robin hood*. Nope.

I sit back. Charlie has hopped out of the bath onto a fluffy dry dish towel. She's rolling around on it and pecking at the terry-cloth loops. She finds a thin thread and pulls. I hear Jacob jangling his keys in the hallway.

Second password: *jaybird*. Nada.

I have one more shot today. I try the one I hope it is: *chlodog*.

The error message pops up: *Access blocked due to too many sign-in attempts. You may try again in 24 hours.*

Crapola. I've started recording my password attempts in my notebook, so I don't waste any attempts on ones I've already tried. Today's three get added to the list.

Charlie finishes drying off and hops onto the edge of my garbage can. She steps onto the swinging lid—

—and flips inside!

"Charlie!" I laugh. I pry the lid off. She's inside on a stack of wadded-up paper, in a nest of homework and art attempts. She flusters her feathers and looks up at me from the bottom of the can.

"Oh no. Cowabunga! Oh no. It's going well! Call 911."

I toss the dish towel over her to keep her from

flapping against the hard plastic can and hurting herself. I scoop her out and place her gently on the desk. She resumes pecking at the loops in the towel.

How in the *world* does this bird know "call 911"?!

I look back at Uncle Will's locked computer. "I need your secrets," I whisper.

"Secrets!" Charlie echoes. *Click-click!* "Secrets!"

But her *call 911* gives me an idea. I snatch up the Post-it note with Deloris's info scrawled on it and punch in the number again. I mean, a good psychic could tell me Will's password, right? Ooo! Or even better, just tell me who the murderer is! Done and done!

The line rings two times, three. Then a froggy voice croaks, "Hello?" A soap opera blares in the background.

I gulp. I was expecting to leave a message. "Is this Deloris?"

"The one and only."

"I . . . uh . . ." I'm totally unprepared for this conversation. "This is Will Calhoun's niece. Chloe."

Deloris mutes the television on her end. Clears her throat. "I know."

I blink. "You do?" Wow, this psychic is good!

Deloris chuckles. It sounds like gravel in a blender. "No, honey. That's a bit of psychic humor."

"Oh." Awkward. I pick at the towel on my desk.

"He . . . uh . . . he passed away. Will. Did you know that?"

Deloris inhales deeply. "I didn't, hon. Not really. I had a dream about it, that he'd passed over. I was hoping it was wrong. I'm sorry, sweetie."

How come so many people don't know when a person has left this earth? It's so weird that it barely blips on the screen for them, while I feel it every minute of every day. Charlie hops into my lap and curls up like she's in a nest. I stroke her head. It gives me the courage to keep asking questions. I'm not sure if my next one is rude.

"Why was Will seeing a psychic?"

I hear a lighter click on Deloris's end of the conversation, and she inhales, exhales. She's a smoker, like Grammy. "I'm a Reiki healer, too. I was helping him manage his pain." A smoker who is a healer. Go figure.

"His pain?" I fight to keep my voice level. Definitely don't want Mom walking in on this conversation. *Who are you talking to, Chloe? Oh, just Will's psychic.* "Was he in a lot of pain?"

Deloris pauses, and I imagine her taking a drag on her cigarette. I wonder what she looks like. I'll have to google her later, because I unfortunately picture her looking like Jabba the Hutt. "I don't think you really want me to answer that question, hon."

"What do you mean? Why not?"

Deloris's voice is even, measured, but as deep as a dark well. "I'm not going to answer that question, because either way, you're going to be unhappy with what I say. If I say he was in pain . . ." Here she exhales what I imagine is a cloud of smoke. ". . . well, that's just sad and terrible, isn't it? But if I tell you he *wasn't* in a lot of pain, then that just raises the question: Why is he gone?"

Why *is* he gone?

Charlie picks *exactly* this moment to blow a raspberry: *bbblllhhhffffttt!* I hope Deloris didn't hear that.

And I don't know what to say, so I just sit there. Unfortunately, I sniffle. Deloris must hear it, because she continues: "Sweetie, seeing a psychic is a lot like seeing a therapist. Will . . . he had some things he needed to work on. I told him he needed to reach back out to you. All of you. His family meant everything to him."

"Did it?" I spit out, before I realize I've said it. Charlie coos in my lap. Deloris is silent.

I try to chuckle, but it comes out sounding like a hard, mean little laugh. "I don't suppose you could tell me the password to Will's computer?"

Deloris chuckles, too, but hers is much more relaxed than my strained laughter. "Oh, hon. I wish. I wish being a psychic worked like that. Imagine how many banks I could rob!"

I can't help it—I laugh. A tear pops out of the corner of my eye, but I don't wipe it away. Sometimes you need to feel a tear streak down your face.

I take another deep breath. "Can you tell me—was Will hurt by someone, or was he sick? It's really important, ma'am."

Deloris shifts on her end, and it sounds like mounds of fabric shift with her. Was she asleep? "Will had a lot of shadows around him. A lot of negativity. Your brother—"

"Uncle," I interrupt her. Seriously, psychic?

"Uncle. He knew a lot of questionable people. He had dangerous folks in his life."

A chill races over my skin, prickling the back of my neck. "Like who?"

Deloris pauses, and it seems like she's weighing her options. "Look, hon. I don't normally talk to others about my clients' lives, you know? I'm like a lawyer or a priest that way."

"I thought you said you were like a psychiatrist."

"Well, a good psychic is like all three." She chortles, which turns into a cough. "Your uncle owed money to some folks. Always said he felt like he was being followed. When I picture Will, I picture him looking over his shoulder, you know? But many of my clients are like that. There's some true paranoia out there. Hard to say when it's warranted and when it's not."

I nod. Being followed. Like by a yellow Prius. Yep. Check.

Deloris keeps going. "He also had some neighbor that was driving him bonkers. Can't remember the guy's name, but he was some hippie from Virginia."

"Boris is from Virginia?!"

"Boris. Hey, yeah. That's the guy." She inhales like she's sucking through a straw. "So, yeah. I'm not saying it was foul play, but I also wouldn't be surprised if it was. Nothing surprises me anymore, sweetheart."

My heart is beating so fast, I feel light-headed and sick.

Do I just . . . hang up?

"Thank you, ma'am."

"Ha! Don't call me ma'am. Makes me feel ancient."

I picture her as ancient, so I don't know what the problem is. "I appreciate you answering my questions."

Inhale, exhale. "No problem, sweetie."

I'm about to hang up when the flash of one last question sparks. "Oh! One more thing. Can you tell me what my future looks like?"

Deloris chuckles or coughs, I'm not sure which. "Sure. For eighty bucks."

I don't reply. Deloris shifts again on her end, and I picture mounds of blankets or skirts shifting with her. She clears her throat. "Chloe," she says, "there's a saying: 'The way I see it, if you want the rainbow, you gotta put up with the rain.' Know who said that?"

My guess doesn't feel right, but I remember a parable about a rainbow from Sunday school. "Is that from the Bible?"

Deloris snorts. "Close. Dolly Parton."

22

THE ANSWER TO EVERYTHING

My head is still spinning from talking to Deloris. That conversation felt like a dream. A nightmare? Something that didn't really happen, either way.

Will felt like he was being followed? Boris is from Virginia? All the pieces are here, but this is one complicated jigsaw puzzle.

"Anybody need anything from the grocery store?" Mom yells upstairs.

"Code Red Mountain Dew!" Jacob shouts back.

"Nope!" Mom replies. "I'll get you a smoothie." Mom's been on this real health kick ever since . . . well . . . Uncle Will. Jacob used to drink that stuff all the time, but not anymore. Which also means I don't get my oatmeal cream pies, either.

Charlie gets excited around loud noises—yelling, horns honking, music, etc. She flusters in my lap, poops on my jeans, and yells, "Tacos! Taco Tuesday!"

I laugh a much-needed laugh. I bend around the doorframe to peek at Mom at the bottom of the stairs. "Charlie wants tacos."

Mom is trying *real hard* not to laugh. She can't yet admit that this bird is stinking adorable. "I heard."

"But seriously," I say. "Baby wipes. Lots of baby wipes. Charlie is . . ." I look at the white-and-brown splotch on my jeans.

"A mess," Mom says. "I know. Okay. Wipes. Text me if you think of anything else. Soccer at four! Grammy's driving you again." Seems like Grammy or Jacob drive me everywhere these days. How did we manage before Jake got his license? How did this work before Grammy moved in? I'm lucky to have options, I guess.

Mom jangles keys, grabs bags, and bangs out of the house. I clean up Charlie's mess and offer her my hand.

Charlie climbs up my arm and perches in my hair. I've learned how to balance her on my head as I walk. She's pretty good at that, ducking and weaving as we bounce downstairs, turn the corner, and head toward the kitchen. I'm feeling lighter already. Just a few words tossed around with my family, and I feel better.

"Want another apple slice, Char?" I ask as we pass through the living room. But Charlie spreads her wings and sails to a cubby in our bookshelves.

Friendly, who was asleep on the back of the couch, wakes up and studies Charlie.

Charlie leans out of the bookshelf and looks up. She hops and flaps, like she's trying desperately to make it to a higher shelf. And then, she *leaps*! She bonks her bird head on the shelf above her and tumbles to the living room rug.

"Charlie!" I scoop her up. She seems a bit dazed, but she's okay. I place her on a higher shelf, hoping that will satisfy her.

It doesn't. She leans out again, looks even higher. She's learned from her last attempt at flying, so she doesn't leap. But she flaps and squawks and tosses a pine cone knickknack off the shelf, letting me know how displeased she is.

Snapshot! I have a sudden memory of Uncle Will plunging both hands deep into our Lego Tupperware bin. I whip out my phone and record the moment: *How many Lego bricks can we stack one by one before it falls over, you think? Fifty? Eighty?*

"Turns out the answer is forty-two," I say into the app. "This made Uncle Will howl with laughter: 'The answer to the ultimate question of life, the universe, and everything is forty-two!' I had no idea what he was talking about or why that was so funny, until he explained that it was a quote from one of his favorite books, *The Hitchhiker's Guide to the Galaxy*."

I get the joke now. I wish the answer to everything was that easy. A silly, random number. But the memory gives me a great idea.

I dig in the back of the coat closet and drag out the Lego bin. Before long, I have an impressive Lego ladder. The ladder reaches from the floor to the very top shelf and stretches out at random heights on both sides.

I lean the ladder against the bookshelf. "Go ahead, Char. This is for you."

She immediately understands how to use the ladder, and I feel a weird swirl of pride at how smart my bird is. Like I had anything to do with her bird brains. She grips the bricks with her claws and climbs higher. And higher still.

"Good girl, Charlie!" I say as she explores each new shelf. "So smart."

"Pretty girl! Pretty bird!" she replies.

I laugh. "Yes, of course. Smart *and* pretty."

Friendly is miffed at this; why can't *she* climb that ladder, too?

"No can do, Friendly," I say. "You weigh twice as much as she does. That ladder won't hold you." She skulks off.

Charlie climbs again to explore the highest shelf.

Dust motes sprinkle down through the sunlight. She sneezes.

"God bless you," I say. "Did your little nares get full of dust?" Nares. Those are bird nostrils. I learned that from *Your African Grey Parrot and You*.

When she climbs back down the Lego ladder, she's covered in dust. She looks like a Swiffer duster. "You be careful," I say. "Don't poop on any books. I'm going to get that apple."

"Where's Will?" she replies. That question—it chips away at my heart a little more every time she asks it. "Wheeeeere's Will?"

I head into the kitchen and wash an apple in the sink. Out of the kitchen window I see— "Yellow Prius!" My heart leaps into my throat and the apple thunks into the silver bowl of the sink. "Jacob! Grammy! Yellow Prius!"

Jacob bounds down the stairs, hopping over the last four. He races to the front door, flings it open, and watches the car whip around the corner.

Grammy rushes in from the hallway bathroom in a cloud of perfume. She scoots up behind Jacob. "It was here? At our *home*?"

Jacob gulps, nods, closes the door. "Yup."

Charlie must get a read on the room because she paces inside a bookshelf cubby, flapping her wings and chattering, "Don't be scared. It's okay. Don't be scared."

Grammy shakes her head at the silver parrot strutting and stuttering on the bookshelf. "I don't want to think my Willie was hurt. But the words that bird knows? I just don't understand . . ." She licks her teeth lightly and grabs her keys. "Chloe, we have to go. I'm dropping you at soccer and then I'm headed to the card game at the senior center. But I'm going to give this some more thought."

My spiral notebook is on the couch, along with my purple sparkly pen. I open the notebook to the list of suspects and add *Driver of a yellow Prius. Virginia plates*. I circle *Virginia* and draw an arrow up to the name *Boring Boris*.

"Boris, maybe you're not so boring after all, huh?"

23

NOT A DUCK!

I grow more and more jittery as the day passes, and I can't sit still. Finally, I go to Jacob's room and knock on the doorframe. "Jay," I say, standing in the doorway, my weight shifting foot to foot. Jacob is doing crunches on his bedroom floor, between a crumpled pair of socks and . . . is that underwear? Ugh.

"Yeah?" he puffs.

"I'm antsy, Jake. Everyone seems like a suspect, and *no one* seems like a suspect."

"I know," he says, and snaps his fingers. "Do some burpees. It'll make you feel better."

I can't ever imagine a scenario where burpees would make me feel *better*. "I have an idea. . . ."

When I tell Jacob that Boris is from Virginia, his

eyes narrow. Ten minutes later, Charlie, Jacob, and I are crammed into his orange muscle car (his words), speeding toward Uncle Will's old apartment.

We luck into a spot underneath Boring Boris's apartment. His blinds are open, and he's inside . . . sleeping? While sitting up?

"Meditating, I think," Jacob mutters. He's leaning forward, peering out of the uppermost portion of his windshield.

"How do you know what meditating looks like?" I murmur. Why are we whispering?

"I mean, it looks like that," Jacob says. He points to the third-story window. Boris sits on a pouf of an ottoman in a patch of sun, eyes closed, legs crossed, hands making tiny Os. "Remember when Dad tried meditating? A few years ago, when he still lived with us. He used to sit just like that."

I snort a laugh. "Dad? Meditating?" I can picture it about as clearly as I can picture Mom skateboarding. Which is to say, not at all.

Jacob grins. "Yeah, he sucked at it. But I liked it. It was ten whole minutes of Mom and Dad not fighting."

I blink. "I don't remember any of that."

Jacob shrugs. "Be glad you don't, Squeak."

He shifts his jaw, and I can tell he's thinking something that he's not saying. "What?" I ask.

"Nothing, just . . ." His shoulders droop a bit.

"Uncle Will and Uncle Frank were really there for us when Dad moved out. I mean, how many uncles coach their niece's soccer team?"

I snort out a *ha!* How could I forget that one awful season when Uncle Will volunteered to coach my soccer team? He knew *nothing* about soccer—NOTHING. Called the pitch a *field*, called our matches *games*. Our coaches had drilled those terms into us for years. "But we had the best team cheer ever," I say.

Jacob lifts his brows. "Are? You? Ready?"

"READY!" I shout. Charlie flaps and ruffles her feathers.

Together, we bounce on Jacob's car seats and clap and holler: "*We don't wear bows! We don't wear skirts! We only wear our soccer shirts! We don't play house! We don't play dolls! We only kick our soccer balls! GOOOOO, LADYBUGS!*"

Charlie squawks loudly, like a big *hurrah!* exclamation point at the end of our fun.

I'm laughing so hard a tear slides down my cheek. "We lost every match but one that season." I pause. "It was also the most fun season I ever had." That was the season when the ice cream dinners began.

We fall into a comfortable silence. I'll record that cheer later in my snapshots.

We peek back at Boring Boris. He's trying to be

still, but he keeps jerking and twitching. Restless.

Guilty?

Suddenly, Boris leaps to his feet and looks out through his blinds.

"Duck!" I yell.

"Not a duck!" Charlie squawks from her pacing path on the back seat. "Not a duck. Pretty girl!"

Jacob and I fling our seats into low-lying positions and sit as still as we can, hiding below the lines of the car windows, as if these measures will keep Boring Boris's eyes off us. Where did humans learn this hiding stuff? Evolution?

A knock on the glass makes my heart leap out of my mouth.

"What the—" Jacob says. He uses the lever on the side of his seat to fling himself upright again. He eases his window down.

George Jones, not the country music singer but Uncle Will's landlord—*former* landlord—leans in. He's holding a dripping garbage bag.

"Can I help you two?" he asks. I can't tell if he's being sarcastic. I decide to take a chance.

"What can you tell us about Will's neighbor?" I ask. I lift my eyebrows at Boring Boris's window.

George follows my gaze to the third story. "That guy? Boris? Never goes anywhere."

Truly Boring Boris.

Jacob's eyes narrow. "So lots of opportunity to get at Will, then."

"*That guy?*" George says again. He chuckles. "Harmless. He's as meek as a lizard." Lizards are meek? "Crabby as heck but harmless."

"How do you know?" I ask. We get out of Jacob's car. Charlie hops up on my elbow, shoulder, head.

"We once had some mice in the building, and he wouldn't let me kill them." George Jones flings his drippy garbage bag into the dumpster next to us. "Talked me into some of those no-harm mousetraps. Those things take forever to work right, but they do work eventually. The one in his apartment was taking MONTHS. Come to find out, he was jamming the trap and letting the mice take all his food. Guy was keeping those rodents as pets! Definitely no killer. Literally couldn't even kill a mouse. Lonely guy, that's all. Not a killer."

We're standing around this dumpster when a low, drawling voice echoes out of the building's crumbling entryway:

"You know who *is* a killer? THAT GODFORSAKEN BIRD!"

24

THIS IS BETTER THAN A TRUE CRIME PODCAST

Jacob, George, and I all spin to see Boring Boris in the doorway to the apartment building. Charlie pivots to stay balanced atop my head. My heart pounds in my ears.

Boris is wearing an oversize maroon hoodie that reads *Virginia Tech*. Jacob slides his eyes at me and nods. *Yep.*

Boris's eyes narrow on Charlie. He lifts a shaky, gnarled hand to point at my parrot and says, "That bird murdered Stuart."

Charlie flaps and flusters. "Awk! It was murder!"

Jacob and I look at each other, and Jacob glances at Charlie. "What?" he says at last.

"Stuart Little!" Boris shouts. People walking on the sidewalk nearby pause and chuckle. "Stuart was my friend, and now he's . . . he's . . ."

George Jones the landlord purses his lips, sighs. "Stuart was one of Boris's mice."

"And that bird *killed him*. At my Christmas party, no less!" Boris's eyes fill with fury. The meditation must not be taking.

George turns to me and Jacob. "Your uncle brought Charlie to the party—"

"I used to love that bird!" Boris shouts, interrupting.

"Pretty bird!" Charlie shouts back, like she's a defendant on the witness stand. I don't know whether to laugh or be upset.

George continues: "And at the party, Charlie spotted one of those mice that Boris wouldn't let me kill."

"IT WAS STUART LITTLE!" Boris booms. A small crowd has gathered on the sidewalk now, listening to the gruesome story of Stuart Little's murder.

"And, well," George continues, his face fighting between laughter and contrition, "Charlie swooped off Will's shoulder. She, uh, *exterminated* Stuart Little."

"That bird murdered my mouse!" Boris shouts, pointing again at Charlie.

"Awk! It was murder!" Charlie fully confesses.

Someone in the crowd mutters, "This is better than a true crime podcast."

"But you tried to break into Will's apartment once," Jacob says. "Kaley told us."

"Yeah!" I chime in. Pathetic, but it's all I got. I add in a mutter, "*Kiley*..."

George Jones blinks at Boris. "You did what?"

Boris's shoulders droop. "I did do that. Because of *that bird*!" Boris's glare at Charlie is downright icy. "Will was gone for the day, and that bird kept asking Alexa to play Def Leppard and Van Halen and Twisted Sister, all sorts of loud, messy hair metal. 'Louder!' she'd say to that machine. 'Alexa, louder!'"

Charlie flusters on my shoulder. She loves music. "Louder!" she says. She claps her beak, *click-click*! "Alexa, louder!"

Boris jabs a crooked finger at her. "Just like that! And that Alexa thing just kept doing it. Getting louder and louder—it sounded like a party thrown by a bunch of rowdy teenagers!"

Jacob guffaws at this and raises his fist to Charlie. Charlie taps it with her claw.

"I tried to break in to unplug that god-awful Alexa. That's all I was trying to do, I swear. Unplug that machine. Stop all that noise. When Will and Kiley walked up on me trying to pick the lock with a nail file, well . . ." Boris gulps. "That was the beginning of the end of my friendship with Will. I think he would've forgiven me for trying to break in, I really do. But it was me who ended the friendship. I just . . . I couldn't get past losing that silly little mouse. I couldn't stop being angry." He's quiet for a moment, then adds in a whisper, "I didn't know Will was sick."

My heart goes out to Boris. I mean, Charlie was just doing what her tiny-bird-brain instincts told her to do: see a mouse, scoop it up. But that mouse meant something to Boris.

I know how painful it is to lose something too soon that means so much to you. My throat tightens.

Boris tugs at the stack of wooden beads around his neck. "But listen, if you are truly looking for someone who might've hurt Will, he owed a bunch of money . . ."

"To a guy named Jaws. We know." Jacob says.

George Jones nods. "I told them that already."

"Do you know anything about this person?" I ask Boris. "We don't know anything other than that . . . nickname." I shudder. I hope it's a nickname. No one would really name their kid Jaws, would they?

Boris swipes a hand down his face, like he's thinking. "Guy owns a restaurant. Don't know the name or where it is. Just that he's in the food business. That's all I know."

Jacob nods. "That's a start. Thanks, bro." Jacob offers Boris his fist, and Boris lights up and bumps it.

Jacob pauses and tips his head at Boris's sweatshirt. "You from Virginia?"

Boris looks down at his hoodie, like he's forgotten what he's wearing. "What? Oh. No. I went to school there. Lived in Charleston my whole life."

We climb into Jacob's car and drive in silence awhile before Jacob says, "Dude doesn't seem likely, does he?"

I shake my head.

Jacob sighs. "Everyone seems like a suspect, and no one seems like a suspect."

25

HEROES

I toss and turn in my bed, punching pillows and tangling sheets, thinking of Boris and Stuart Little, thinking about who drives a yellow Prius, thinking about what a person named *Jaws* might look like. As for that last one: none of the folks I picture are lovely. Most of them have pointy teeth and metal appendages. Hooks. Scars.

When we got home from our stakeout, Jacob and I reported back to Uncle Frank and Grammy what we learned: Boring Boris seems unlikely to be our guy. Jaws owns a restaurant. People are entertained by the murder of a mouse named Stuart Little.

A box of Uncle Will's stuff still sits in the corner of my room. I dig out the six decks of cards and stack them, building a tiny house with a walkway leading up to it. A true house of cards is built card by card; it's flimsy and fragile. This one is made of cards, but it feels chunky, like a log cabin. Somehow the sturdiness of this paper comforts me, and I like the idea that two things that are opposite can both be true.

Fresh off my night of very little sleep, I trudge through school, purple bags under my eyes and yawns between every sentence. ("You look like death," Audrey says, and hugs my neck.) Finally, at long last, I land in my chair in art class.

"Friends!" Ms. Umar sings. "It is almost the end of the school year! Can you believe it? That means it's time for . . ." She drumrolls her palms on the tops of her legs. ". . . our final project!"

Most of the class groans. I want to groan, too, but not because we have a project ahead. I want to groan because it's the final one. I love this class.

Ms. Umar turns to the whiteboard and writes in huge, perfect script: *Hero*.

"That's our theme, class: hero. I want you to paint a portrait of your hero."

More groans. One kid murmur-sings, *"There goes my hero . . ."*

"And wait—it gets better!" Ms. Umar continues. "I will pick three paintings from our school to be represented at the district-wide art competition!"

She stands with her arms wide, her smile wider. Her gold earrings sway like flames. Her excitement fills the room like rays of sunlight.

Everyone's excited now, basking in the sunshine of Ms. Umar's announcement. The district-wide art competition is a big deal. The first-place prize is two hundred fifty dollars, given by some local foundation whose goal is to pay artists for art. Two hundred fifty dollars! That's, like, months in a manatee outfit.

Is it possible for a heart to leap and sink at the same time? The district-wide art competition! I want this so bad I can taste it. *Want* tastes like lemon: sweet and tart. I can't imagine doing this, actually being a part of the *district-wide art competition*.

But I know for sure who I'm painting. My hero?
Uncle Will.

The district-wide art competition. The big leagues. At home, I decide to block in the colors for the painting right away. This one is going to take time, and I want to get it right.

I set up an easel in the living room, where the light is best. I squeeze just three dots of paint on my pallet. I scoop up dollops of pink and yellow with a wide, flat brush and "X" the paint across the canvas. It's a soft peachy-coral color, with flashes of yellow bursting through. It reminds me of lemonade. Lemons. Sweet and tart. The perfect backdrop for Uncle Will.

My phone rings, and Charlie squawks in excitement. She loves FaceTime, loves seeing herself on camera. The call is from Audrey. I hesitate, because all I really want to do is paint. But that's what carpe diem is all about, right? Cramming everything in all at once. I can paint and take care of Charlie and chat with Audrey before heading to soccer and doing homework. Carpe-flipping-diem! I've been blowing her off way too much lately. "Hey!" I can hear how flat my voice sounds.

"Hey! Let's paint together!" she says.

I smile weakly. "Okay." I prop the phone against my paintbrush cup. "Charlie will likely want to show you her butt."

"Hi, Charlie!" Audrey says, waving hello with her paintbrush. "I'd love to see your bird butt!"

Charlie says *awk* and paces in front of the phone, showing off her beauty. Audrey laughs. "Hi, pretty girl!"

Charlie pecks at the phone screen. "Pretty girl! Pretty Charlie!"

Painting. I need to focus on painting.

We're both silent, looking at our own creations, dabbing paint here and there. I swipe a misplaced glob of paint off my canvas and try another color. Ugh. Still too peachy for Uncle Will's skin. I huff.

"Do you ever watch murder mysteries?" I ask

without really thinking. "Do they freak you out?"

"I love the movie *Clue*!" Audrey cocks her head at her painting. "But it's not really scary. It's more . . . goofy. Why?"

Jaws. The Yellow Prius. Birds cawing *It was murder.* Chill bumps creep over my skin. But I shrug. "No real reason. Looking for my next Netflix binge."

"Rom. Coms," Audrey says. She turns back to her painting and dabs on more Clemson orange.

"Your sister?" I ask, pointing my paintbrush at the camera.

Audrey beams. "Yep! Katherine, of course. Not Lindsey. Linds would die of embarrassment if I painted her. Katherine's semester is over next week. She'll be home and will wait tables again."

"Going back to Cheesecake Factory?"

Audrey taps her paintbrush handle on her lips and shakes her head. "No, a local place. The Shark's Den, I think? It's her old boss, though. Katherine says everyone in the restaurant business knows each other."

I almost drop my paintbrush. Charlie flusters and plucks feathers from near her tail. "They do?"

Audrey shrugs and paints a blue paw print on the orange shirt. "Yeah. They follow each other around from place to place, Katherine says. It's like a cult, restaurant workers."

"Could you . . ." My voice suddenly dries up, and

Audrey senses the conversation has turned. She looks at the camera. A FaceTime crime, really, the direct gaze.

"Yeah?"

"Could you ask her if she knows a guy named Jaws?"

Audrey's eyebrows shoot up. "Jaws? Really?"

I try to laugh it off, like the name doesn't terrify the bejeezus out of me. "Yeah. Huh. It's a guy my uncle used to know. I'd like to find him." I turn back to my painting and try to appear nonchalant.

"You sure your uncle wasn't in the mafia?" Audrey laughs.

"I'd believe just about anything these days," I mutter. But I fake-laugh, too, and tack on a fake smile for good measure. "Can you ask?"

Audrey shrugs. "Sure. I'll text her right now."

I stand back, trying to decide on the next layer. Yellow? Red? No color seems brilliant enough to fully capture Uncle Will. My phone pings. I figure it's Dad, telling me what I should focus on in soccer practice tonight. He texts before every practice and calls after for a recap. But when I flip the phone over, it's Audrey. Wow, she works fast! It's only been about twenty minutes since our call. My heart races and I swallow past a huge lump in my throat as I text Jacob, Uncle Frank, and Grammy:

I found Jaws.

26

JAWS DON'T PLAY NICE

SoccerPractice > MoreHomework > RestlessSleep > TossAndTurn > WakeUp > Breakfast > SchoolSchoolSchool > MoreSoccerUgh > ThenFINALLYHOME.

I am a jittery mess by the time late afternoon gets here. We have plans to finally, FINALLY go see Jaws. I'm pacing the living room floor, waiting. Charlie shuffles to the edge of her cage and—*ping!*—makes a noise that sounds just like an iPhone getting a text. I double-check my phone to make sure it wasn't really a message. Nope—all Charlie.

In the kitchen, Mom picks up her phone, too. She cocks her head at the blank screen, shrugs, puts her phone down, and keeps cutting coupons.

I giggle, and it helps my nervousness. "Charlie, when did you learn that?"

"*Ping!*" Charlie says again. "*Ping! Ping!*" It sounds like an onslaught of texts.

Mom turns over her phone again. The screen is still blank. She purses her lips but places her phone back down and continues cutting.

Charlie kicks up one claw, then the other, and makes a noise that sounds exactly like an iPhone ring: "*Do do do dooo, do do do dooo, do do do dooo, doooooo.*"

Mom snatches up her phone. Nothing. It's not ringing. "Errrgghhhh!" she says. Then she squints at me and Charlie over the kitchen island.

"Charlie, you troll!" I laugh-whisper. Charlie bobs and weaves, and I swear she's giggling.

"That bird!" Mom shouts. "UGH! I need some fresh air." She leaps off the stool and flings open the door.

Uncle Frank is there, fist lifted like he was *just* about to knock.

He startles. "Uh, hello?"

Mom shouts, "That bird!" and pushes past him out the door.

Uncle Frank chuckles at her backside, marching away. Then he turns to me, and his face gets serious.

Deadly serious.

"Ready to go see Jaws?"

I nod. Uncle Frank looks over his shoulder, out the front door, to see where Mom went. "Get the others," he whispers, and jerks his head toward Mom as she stomps down the driveway. "But . . . you know . . ."

I nod again. "Don't tell Mom. She'd freak out."

We're in Uncle Frank's car: Grammy riding shotgun and applying red lipstick like she's about to meet the queen, and Jacob, me, and Charlie in the back. It's getting dark now, and the streetlights shimmer. Headlights sweep through the dark, quiet car. It's creepy, the shadows that crawl behind the beams of light.

I read aloud the text that Audrey sent me, and the text that her sister sent *her*:

I asked around about Jaws. My old coworker Caitlyn says Jaws owns this place called Shorty's. She also says, and I quote, "DON'T MESS WITH JAWS. JAWS DON'T PLAY NICE."

"Shorty's," Uncle Frank says, eyeing Charlie in the rearview mirror. He's so worried about Charlie's poop. But I have wipes. "Will used to play cards there."

"Kind of a pool hall, right?" Grammy says. "Over by the marina on Shipyard Creek."

"Yep," Uncle Frank says. "Will once told me he owed someone there money. I thought he meant from a card game. You know, like a couple hundred bucks or something. But maybe not? Maybe he meant more?"

His forehead wrinkles deeper in the rearview mirror, and I get the feeling it's not about Charlie anymore. "Couple years ago, Will would've asked me to cover that debt. He always said he'd pay me back. He . . ."

Never did. Uncle Frank doesn't say those two words, but they hang in the air anyway. He's working his jaw back and forth so hard, I'm surprised we can't hear his teeth squeak. "I should never have cut him off. What did it hurt me to keep forking out a couple hundred bucks here and there? But I did. I told him no more. 'I'm not going to keep paying for your stupid choices at the poker table,' I said. 'You're the older brother. Act like it.' I told my own brother that."

Uncle Frank doesn't even seem to remember we're all here in the car with him. He drives for a bit, then gives his head a quick shake like he's waking up. "Doesn't play nice, huh?" The shadows keep chasing the light through his car.

As we get closer and closer to Jaws, the tension in the car grows. I can practically hear the music from the movie *Jaws* pulsing at us now. It feels like an old-school rubber band on your arm, getting pulled tighter and tighter, and *man*, is it going to hurt when it snaps back against your wrist.

Grammy licks her teeth. "I want to talk to that gentleman."

Jacob squints and cracks his knuckles. "Me too."

Uncle Frank grinds his jaw. "Me too."

Charlie clicks her beak twice like a double-snap and squawks, "Me too! Me too!"

I can't help it. I laugh. It breaks the tension, and soon we're all laughing. And we laugh and laugh, and Charlie bobs and weaves, and it feels perfect and loud and joyous until somehow, for some reason, the cup overflows and all that laughter turns dark, and now we have tears pricking our eyes. All four of us, bleary-eyed and silent. We're scared.

The snap of the rubber band. It stings.

We pull into the gravel lot at Shorty's. Or not gravel but ground-up shells and sand. The building looks like it will *not* survive the next hurricane season. It's a bunch of weathered gray boards nailed together, and a rusty sign squeaks in the wind overhead: *Sh t s*. Half the neon letters have blown out. Jacob and Uncle Frank are obviously filling in the blanks with their own letters, because they point at the sign and bump shoulders and their faces pull into smirks.

I can always count on those two to bring the body humor.

Shorty's is huge, though, sprawling over several sand dunes, and dozens of cars and motorcycles dot the lot, even on a Wednesday night. A Lynyrd Skynyrd song pulses out of the building, along with the smell of stale cigarette smoke. Charlie, on my shoulder, caws, "Alexa, play 'Freebird'!" She whistles a few bars of the song, but we're all too wound up to laugh.

We eye each other and inhale, like we're about to dive underwater. Where Jaws lives.

27

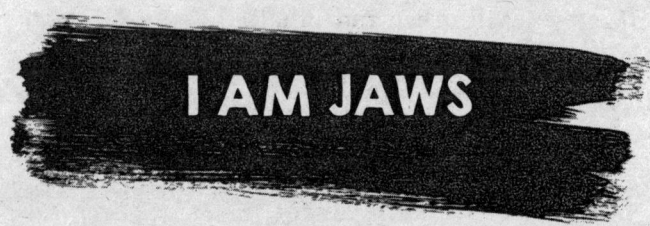
I AM JAWS

The door into Shorty's is dark, smoky glass, and it's heavy. It takes all my might to push it open. Inside, it's dim—the only light comes from neon beer signs—and smells like a moldy sponge. The crack of balls on a pool table sounds like the crunch of bones, and I shiver as we walk in.

We stand out like we're wearing clown suits to church. But no one pays us any attention. Even though I have a huge parrot on my shoulder. Even though Jacob and I are far too young to be here. There are a few poker games going on toward the back of the room, but the players are too busy shuffling cards and clinking chips to size us up. The sounds of the cards and chips boosts my determination: *We are here for Uncle Will.*

I can see him in my mind, smiling at me across the green expanse of a poker table: *Time to ante up, Chlodog.*

"Uh, how long are we going to stay here?" Jacob whispers, his eyes scanning this place. "I think I just saw a dude open a Coke bottle with his teeth."

"That wasn't a Coke bottle," Uncle Frank and Grammy say in unison. Grammy adds, "And it wasn't a dude."

We scan the bar for Jaws. I don't know what we expect, like maybe this particular loan shark will be wearing a name tag that reads *Hello, My Name Is Jaws.* Our eyes adjust to the dark and the smoke, and our gazes fall on the bartender.

Massive guy. Big, burly, bald, and tattooed. Studded leather vest, no shirt underneath. He certainly fits the nickname. Uncle Frank gulps, and we approach him.

"Are you Jaws?" Uncle Frank asks. Too loudly. Suddenly, every eye in the place looks our way. Did the music just drop in volume?

The guy is wiping out a glass. It looks so small in his huge mitts, like he could crush it with a flex of his fingers. He squints at us, and his gaze falls on Charlie, perched on my shoulder. I shrink back.

"Who's asking?" he growls.

Grammy steps forward, tugging at the hem of her blazer. "We're here about Will Calhoun."

Whispers rise from everyone inside this joint like tiny poofs of dust. A chair scratches across the floor. The bartender puts down the glass and loops the dish towel around his thick neck. The towel barely reaches over both shoulders.

"Ma!" he shouts into the kitchen behind him. "Ma! Some folks are here to see Jaws!"

"All right, all right!" a voice shouts back. The kitchen door swings wide, and at first I don't see her around the height of the bar. A small, gray-haired woman totters out. A pair of reading glasses hangs around her neck on a beaded chain. She lifts them to her face and peers over their rim at us. The burly bartender leans over her, whispering something. All I can make out is *Will Calhoun*.

"Rose?" the woman says, blinking at Grammy.

"Mildred!" Grammy says. For once, Grammy is speechless. The two women are locked in a staring contest.

I lean over to Jacob, shifting the weight of Charlie on my shoulder. "Mildred?" I whisper. "How do I know that name?"

Jacob looks just as confused as I feel. "She's the woman who cheats at bridge at the senior center."

Grammy blinks a few times, shaking off her stupor. "Mildred, you know Jaws?"

Mildred chuckles and crosses her arms over her chest. Half her face lifts in a witchy scowl. "Rose, darling. I *am* Jaws."

28

FIVE-CARD CHARLIE

Grammy purses her lips, taking a long time to think about what might come next. She can't help herself: she snorts. "Doesn't surprise me that you're a loan shark," she blurts at last. I cringe.

Mildred lays her fingertips on her chest, pretending to be offended. "I'm not a loan shark, Rose. I'm . . . an investor. A *community* investor. An entrepreneur."

Grammy looks so perturbed, I think she might yank off her earrings and put this Mildred woman in a headlock. "Is that why you gave yourself the name Jaws?"

Mildred looks smug. "Some nicknames just stick."

Uncle Frank gently positions himself between Grammy and Mildred, but Grammy is having none of it. She leans around Uncle Frank. "Did you kill my son?"

The sentence hangs there in the air, stinking and gray like cigarette smoke.

My heart beats like thunder. Fear pulls me out of myself, and suddenly, I'm picturing a snapshot of me and Uncle Will, strolling along Folly Beach. He points at a boat—a huge, ugly, rusty barge—and says, *If you could escape to anywhere, where would you go?*

He was a master of escape, Uncle Will. A regular Houdini.

I'm learning? That's not always a good thing.

Do I record those snapshots, too? Should I record the less-than-stellar memories along with the great ones? Do I want to remember all of him, or just the good parts?

Charlie nibbles at the top of my ear, reminding me to be *here, now*. I shake off the memory.

Did Mildred's face soften ever so slightly? She purses her wrinkled lips. "I didn't kill the guy. No offense, but I knew it would happen soon. Guy was real sick. That genetic disease sounded terrible. Why would I risk getting caught if he's going to kick it soon anyways?"

I notice she's not offended by the question, though.

Grammy's fists knot, and if she were a cartoon character, steam would be shooting out her ears. Uncle

Frank steps fully between the two women.

Mildred is unaffected by my grammy's anger. "Listen. If I off a mark, I don't get paid. That don't make any sense. I don't get paid if the guy dies, see. I'm a good businesswoman. I want to get paid." Mildred removes her reading glasses and polishes them with the hem of her cardigan. "Unless, of course, his dumb relatives come looking for me. Then *they* owe me his debts. Understand?"

She smirks as she places her glasses on the tip of her nose, waiting for what she's saying to sink in: Now *we* are in debt to her. *We* owe her the money Uncle Will borrowed from her, because we came asking about it. George Jones even warned us this would happen. How dumb can we be!

Jaws lifts her chin at Uncle Frank's wrist. "That a Rolex?" Her tone isn't subtle: *I know you have money.* "That sure would look nice on my grandson here." She elbows the hulking guy in the leather vest. He nods.

Uncle Frank crosses his arms to hide his shiny watch. He grinds his jaw so hard, I imagine his molars are turning to dust. "How much are we talking?" he asks through gritted teeth.

Jaws says a number so big, I can hardly wrap my brain around it.

Jacob leans back and gives the moment a long, low

whistle. Charlie does the same. That would normally be adorable, but now it just seems to highlight how big the number really is. Uncle Will owed so much money! "That's as much as a new car," Jacob mutters to me.

I can suddenly taste the chemical smell of Uncle Frank's new SUV. And there he stands, jingling the keys in his pocket like he can taste it, too. My eyes lock with Grammy's. She's thinking the same thing.

Uncle Frank *cannot* give Jaws his car key. Because he would do that. Uncle Frank would do that if it meant he could keep the rest of us safe and out of this mess.

Grammy crosses her arms and glares at Jaws. "We're not paying."

Did everyone in this joint collectively gulp? Or was my own gulp just that huge? Jaws smirks and looks up at the burly bartender, who twists his neck from side to side: *crack, crack!* Charlie claps her beak and imitates the head twist. The bartender grins, and I'm surprised to see a mouth full of braces. Metal teeth. I shiver.

Jaws lights up suddenly. It's weird, watching her face transform like that, like it's made out of hot wax. "How about this, Rose? How about a quick game of blackjack? You win, all debts are off. I win . . . you pay."

Oh, this woman knows *exactly* how to get Grammy's goat. A game of twenty-one. Grammy flares her nostrils. "You're on."

The people at the nearest poker table scatter like dust bunnies under a huff of breath. Grammy sweeps into one chair, and Jaws plops into the one opposite her. "My son Frank will deal," Grammy says lightheartedly.

Smart move. Uncle Frank, the magician. With his sleight of hand, he can make sure Grammy gets the exact cards she needs.

Jaws scowls, her waxy face melting toward the floor again. "Don't be ridiculous. If he's anything like Will, he's got aces in his underwear."

Jacob snorts a laugh. I elbow him.

Jaws must see me do that, because she cocks her head at me. "No," she says, and lifts a crooked, shaky finger at me and Charlie. "Her. She's the dealer."

The back of my neck prickles. Every eyeball in the place is on me. Charlie must feel the attention, because she shuffles and squawks, "Pretty bird! Say please and thank you!"

Grammy shakes her head, but I sit between the two of them. "Okay," I say, and I squeeze Grammy's hand. "For Uncle Will."

Jaws squints at me. "This is blackjack, sweetie. Each of us gets two cards—"

Grammy waves her off. "She knows."

I shuffle the cards, slick and smooth. Toss them to

and fro between my hands in a clattering waterfall. Spread them across the table and flip them in one long line. Cut the deck in the palm of one hand and tuck it behind the other. Jaws raises her eyebrows at my shuffling skills.

Blackjack. The goal is to get as close to twenty-one as you can without going over. Easy, right? I deal Grammy a card, face down, then one to Jaws. Then I slide Grammy a card, face up. Same to Jaws.

Grammy shows a two. Jaws, an ace.

In other words, the worst possible hand for Team Will. The crowd moans. "Traitors," Jaws mutters at them, and shuffles in her seat.

Grammy peeks at the corner of her face-down card. "Hit me," she says. I sling another card her way. It's another two. She has four showing. Interesting. I look to Jaws.

She's smug. "I'll stay," she says, waving her hand *no* over her two cards. Crud. That likely means she has blackjack. Twenty-one. Her ace that's showing is worth eleven. She likely has a ten or a face card hidden.

Grammy doesn't blink. "Hit me," she says again, tapping the table. Her hidden card must be low, too, and she's working toward a 5-Card Charlie! A 5-Card Charlie is a loophole hand: if you can gather five cards and the total is *less than* twenty-one, it wins, beating all other hands.

It *has* to be good luck that she's working toward a 5-Card Charlie and we *have* a Charlie, right?

I fling another card her way, face up. It's a six. She now has ten showing, with four cards. All she needs is one more low card. . . .

She licks her teeth.

Her tell. Oh no. That's not good. She's going to chance it.

Jacob bounces on his toes next to me. Uncle Frank works his jaw. Charlie floats to the green felt table and scoots a poker chip off the edge. It clatters to the floor; it's so quiet in here, it sounds as loud as a car crash.

"Hit me," Grammy says again. It's like slow motion, watching her tap the tabletop. I fling another card her way, face up.

The queen of spades. Ten. Grammy groans, "Noooo!" and flips over her hidden card: a four. Twenty-four. She busted.

My heart sinks. I didn't deal the right cards. I feel sick. I failed my family.

Jaws's waxen face lights up again and morphs into a scowl. She flips her hidden card. It's a two.

She only has thirteen. If Grammy had stopped before that last card, she would've won by *one*.

Uncle Frank digs in his pants pocket and rattles his key fob. He's ready to hand over his car right now.

Jacob looks like he's about to jump out of his skin, he so desperately wants Uncle Frank to keep that new car of his. "What happens if we just don't pay?"

If it was silent in here before, it's like a tomb now. Mildred's lips curl, and her smirk highlights how she got the nickname Jaws. She steps toward Jacob, her breath smelling like hours of coffee.

"This kind of debt is like DNA, see," she says to Jacob. Her voice is low, like a drum. "It passes from one family member to the next. It's a disease, and it'll kill each of you."

It's a horrible, awful, terrible thing to say to a family who just lost someone to a genetic disease.

Supposedly lost someone to a genetic disease. It's feeling less and less like that's what really happened.

29

DON'T BE HASTY

Grammy stands, her chair screeching against the dirty linoleum floor. She grabs Uncle Frank's elbow, her signal to him: *Don't be hasty*. "When is this money due, *Mildred*?"

Jaws stands, laughs, and elbows the bartender. The burly dude knows to copy her laugh and he chuckles, too. "Get a load of this one," she guffaws. "'*Due*,' she says. DUE? We're not a library, Rose."

Up to this point, Jaws has looked like an irritable old biddy, maybe uncomfortable because she has a wedgie or something, but not evil. But her face shifts again, eyes narrowed, bottom jaw locked. She leans toward my grandmother, and meanness radiates off her like an electric shock.

Grammy does not lean back.

"The money is due *now*, Rose," Jaws says. "Now. It was *due* two months ago. So yeah, it's due now. But I'll give you five days."

Grammy smacks her lips defiantly. "Five days? You've got to be kidding."

Jaws cocks her head, and her glasses slip down her nose. "Now you get three. Keep it up, Rose."

Jacob is the first one to collect his senses. He elbows Uncle Frank and lifts his chin toward the door. The four of us—five, with Charlie—walk silently toward the exit before Jaws can strip us of any more days. The jukebox plays an old country music song, one that Uncle Will used to love: *She got the gold mine. I got the shaft.*

Jacob is pushing the door open, but he stops short. His eyes widen, and he grabs my wrist.

"Yellow Prius!" he shouts, and points right at it.

We all whip our heads out the door and look to the left, following the direction of his point.

The car must realize we've spotted it because it spins its wheels, tossing sand and shells over a row of motorcycles before swerving out of the lot and down the street.

"Who *is* that?" I ask.

"Definitely a suspect," Jacob says, eyes still on the cloud of dust left behind by the Prius. "He's everywhere."

Grammy turns her phone to face us. She snapped a photo of the yellow Virginia license plate. It's fuzzy, but readable. "Don't know. But maybe we can find out."

Jaws scoots over and breathes down our necks, craning to look at the phone screen, too. "Getting tailed, huh? Ugh. The worst."

She says this like it happens every day, like, "Eh, a cavity," or "Oops, yeah, paper cuts are awful."

Grammy narrows her eyes at Jaws, who looks more like a Mildred again. "You know who this is? Is this one of your goons?"

"Goons." Mildred chuckles. "You watch too much TV, Rose." She adjusts her reading glasses and squints at Grammy's phone. "Not one of mine. But I can find out who it is. Send me that photo."

Uncle Frank looks skeptical. "Why would you do that for us?"

Mildred removes her glasses. "I told you, I'm a smart businesswoman. Call it extra incentive for you to pay up. You pay me in three days, and I'll have the name of the guy driving that electrified piece of tin." She looks at me and Jacob. Her gaze makes Charlie shiver on my shoulder.

"Plus, it sounds like information you really want to know. A *suspect*? That's info you'd pay for."

Grammy shrugs and texts the photo to Jaws,

muttering, "If we're paying anyway, we might as well get a name."

The car ride home is silent. We're all thinking about paying off Jaws, getting the name of the guy in the Prius. Jacob squirms and says at last, "I'll get the manatee job back. Help chip in."

Grammy appears to be calculating things in her head. "I've got a little savings I can use. I hate the thought of my money ending up in that woman's bank account, but I want to be done with this."

Uncle Frank shakes his head. "I'll take care of it. I can handle it." His wide, shiny SUV suddenly feels smaller, duller. He was so proud of it just thirty minutes ago. Now it feels like we're riding around in someone else's car.

Grammy reaches toward him and lays her hand over his on the steering wheel. "We don't want you to do that. A family isn't one person."

Jacob and I nod. It's true. Uncle Frank shouldn't have to be the only one out here cleaning up Uncle Will's mess.

I'm thirteen years old, so job opportunities aren't exactly flinging themselves at my feet. But I do know one way I can earn some money to help.

I can win the all-district art show. I can get two

hundred fifty dollars and give it to Uncle Frank to help pay off Uncle Will's debt. It's not a lot, but I want to help. I am the one who led us to Jaws, after all.

Charlie seems to feel my growing nervousness. She flusters her wings and hops onto the headrest behind me.

Uncle Frank flicks his eyes up to the rearview mirror. "If that bird poops in here, don't clean it up. If I'm giving this car to Jaws, let's leave her a little extra gift, huh?"

30

DOESN'T WANT TO BE FOUND

By the time we get home, Grammy has worked herself into a tizzy. She's a woman on a mission now. I pity whoever is on the other side of Grammy's wrath, and I'm grateful that her spite is on my team. She heads straight to the family laptop in the living room and starts searching.

"I don't trust Mildred as far as I can throw her," Grammy says, squinting at the computer monitor. "I'm going to dig a little on this license plate, too. Keep that woman honest."

Jacob nods. "I'll help." He hovers over Grammy's shoulder while she types, and she keeps swatting his hand away. "I *know* what a browser is, Jacob." But she pauses before she clicks on the correct icon.

They type and argue, argue and type. The three of us are in the living room, on the family laptop, adrenaline still pumping after our meeting with Jaws.

"You don't have to type in 'how do I find someone when I have their full license plate number,' Grammy," Jacob says. "You can just type—"

Grammy's lips flatten. "I used to be a girl Friday, Jacob. Don't tell me how to type."

Jacob widens his eyes at me and shrugs. "I don't even know what that means." I laugh, and my heart swells. This whole thing reeks like a fishing wharf on a hot summer day, but my family—they're really helping me with this!

Meanwhile, I swing open Will's laptop and try three more passwords:

Jaws

Charlie

Virginia

Nope, nope, nope.

Locked out.

Crud. I toss the laptop onto the couch and record the password attempts in my notebook.

Charlie waddles into the kitchen and squawks, so I lift her onto the island. I can tell she feels so vulnerable when she's on the ground. Feeling vulnerable is the worst. Jaws is showing my family that right now.

While Grammy and Jacob argue over Google Chrome, I decide to try the next layer of my hero painting. The painting that I need to win two hundred fifty dollars to help with Uncle Will's debts to a loan shark. So we can get the name of the goon who is tailing us. No pressure. Charlie struts across the kitchen island, knocking off the salt and pepper shakers, ripping paper napkins to shreds. I block in the next layer of paint: Will's head.

"'Try to build a painting rather than paint it,'" Ms. Umar said earlier this week. "An artist named Chuck Close said that. Build your paintings, class. Step by step. Layer by layer. It's a journey."

Build your painting. I stand back and tap the end of the paintbrush against my lips. This portrait is actually looking good! I mean, you can tell it's going to be a human, so . . . win?

Grammy pushes the rolling chair away from the desk. Her scowl is deep. "Well, that tells us nothing!"

"What? What did you find?" I ask, attention torn away from the portrait. My attention these days is like those napkins Charlie is ripping apart. Is that a side effect of carpe-ing the diem? Seizing every moment of a day?

Jacob shakes his head. He has Grammy's phone

open to the photo of the license plate. "These orange and white stickers," he says, and points to two small squares on the bottom of the plate, "show it's a rental car."

"A rental car?" I say, squinting at the phone. "What does that mean?"

"It means we can't track down the driver," Grammy says. "Not easily, at least. Probably not legally. Doubtful Mildred can get a name, either. They did a whole episode on crimes committed in rental cars on *WHO-DUNNIT*. Trust me. Whoever is following us is *good*. They don't want to be found."

Charlie looks sleepy, tucking her head under her wing. She murmurs, "Where's Will?"

"I wish I knew," I whisper. I place her gently in her cage and head upstairs to my room. I fling my spiral notebook and my purple sparkle pen on the bed, leap onto the mattress, and open the notebook to the well-worn page that reads *Suspects!*

My pen hovers over the page. I scan each person. Uncle Frank and Kiley the ex, both scratched through. I finally scratch through George Jones the landlord and Boring Boris in number 13, too—my instinct tells me they are both a *no*. Jaws? She says she didn't do it because she wanted payment. But can someone like that truly be trusted? She stays on the list. Driver of a Yellow Prius. I add there: *Rental car. Doesn't want to be found.*

I run my finger over where I've scratched through *Uncle Frank*. Guy was about to fork over the keys to his brand-new SUV today, no questions asked. I still don't have any proof other than my heart telling me he didn't do it. But I figure that's as good a proof as any.

I'm so jumpy. Antsy. I can't really remove anyone else from this list. Not yet. Not without that stupid laptop password. The last two suspects remain there on the list, taunting me.

I hear Mom bang inside the house, her symphony as always the sound of shuffling plastic bags and keys clanging in the key bowl.

"Chloe, soccer!"

What? "I thought we had today off!" I shout back. Maybe Coach called an extra practice this week. We *are* about to head into the final part of the season.

"Chloe! Chloe soccer!"

"All right, all right, I hear you!" I gather up my gear as quickly as I can and cram it into a bag. Crap, I don't have anything together! I sniff a pair of shorts—not totally awful—and pull them on quickly. Socks and shin guards and cleats . . . rush rush rush, go go go!

"Chloe!"

"I hear you! I'm coming!" I shout, tumbling down the stairs. I look at Mom, who stands in the middle of the living room, tears streaming down her face. My heart plummets. What now?! Did Jaws do this?

"Mom, are you—"

Mom gasps. Bends in half, hands on knees.

Then I realize: She's *laughing*. Not crying.

Mom points at Charlie.

"Chloe!" Charlie chirps. "Soccer! Time to go!"

I look from Mom, gasping for air, to Charlie, fluttering her wings like laughter, like she knows exactly how much she's made me rush. I scowl, trying hard not to laugh myself.

I toss the bag at the base of the cage. "Thanks a bunch, Charlie!"

"Whoooo!" Mom exhales at last. As I'm stomping back up the stairs, I hear her say, "Thanks, bird. I needed that."

A bit later, I hear Mom talking to herself in the living room. That's not all that unusual—moms do that all the time. But I hear her say, "Will," and my curiosity gets the best of me. I creep halfway down the stairs and listen.

Mom is sweeping dusty birdseed off our laminate wood floor. I quickly realize she's not talking to herself, though.

"I do miss him, Charlie," she says. She grunts a bit as she bends over the dustpan. "I bet you do, too, huh, girl?"

"Pretty girl," Charlie says. She plucks a feather from near her right leg.

"He was the most impulsive son of gun you'll ever meet," Mom says with a chuckle. She plops onto the cushiony ottoman. "Like this one time. A neighbor kid was making fun of Frank for doing his magic tricks, you know? Called him a dork. Typical mean-kid stuff. And Will . . ."

Mom hangs her head, her elbows on her knees, and she looks more tired than I've ever seen her look. When she raises her head, her eyes glisten. A rare thing for my mom.

"Will put this kid in a headlock, see. He forced that kid to sit through a whole magic show of Frank's. Frank was *pissed*, too. But he was mad about the wrong thing!" Mom snorts, then changes her voice in what I guess is an attempt to sound like Uncle Frank: "'I don't want to do magic for someone who doesn't truly appreciate the art form, Will!'"

Mom spits out another laugh. "Frank wasn't pissed about Will fighting his battles for him at all—and that's the part that got me riled up. I tried to get Frank mad about that. I tried to get Will to see how he couldn't just fight all of Frank's enemies. But they looked at me like I had two heads when I said they were both wrong. Like an older brother watching out for a younger brother was the most natural thing in the world."

"Wrong!" Charlie squawks. "She was wrong!" Huh. That's a new one.

Mom squints at Charlie. "I never once thought that maybe *I* was the one who was wrong."

Mom sighs, and her body heaves. She's not crying, but she's as close to it as you can be minus actual sobs.

"I feel like I'm made of ninety-nine hearts, and every one of them hurts."

It takes my breath away, how so many feelings rush in, overhearing my mom say that. I clench my fists, my teeth, and whisper, "I will find out what happened, Uncle Will. Your killer is not going to get away with hurting you *and* all of us, too."

31

IS PROTECTION ALWAYS LOVE?

"Chloe, soccer!" a voice shouts up the stairs.

Today, unlike yesterday, it's true: I do have soccer, and Grammy is the one hauling us there.

Us. I'm finally bringing Charlie to meet the team! I have to do *something* to keep my friends from getting too suspicious. I've blown them off too much lately. Lydia told me yesterday that I've been acting weird, and earlier this week, Emmi squeezed me too hard and asked if I was mad at her. This investigation is taking up all my time.

I lower my paintbrush. I've moved the painting of Will back up to my room. There comes a point in making a piece of art that feels very personal. The painting is beginning to *feel* real, even beginning to look like

Uncle Will, and I don't like having my heart sitting out in the open, thumping in the middle of our living room.

Plus, there's the added pressure of *needing* to win the all-district art competition. That money hangs over my head like a cartoon anvil on a dinky little rope. Money = name of another suspect. Money = helping Uncle Frank. I won't get the prize money until after Jaws has been paid off—the money is now due in *two days!*—but I can give it to Uncle Frank as a thank-you. Chip in. Do my part. That's what family does.

"Chloe, honey, we need to leave!"

I rush to dunk paintbrushes in water and cap all my acrylic paints.

"Chloe!"

"I'm coming!" I huff. *Carpe diem, carpe diem, carpe diem . . .*

We pile into Grammy's red Mustang convertible, and Grammy is irked when I remind her that *no*, we can't put the top down with Charlie in the car. Grammy looks tired. Big-puffy-purple-bags-under-her-eyes tired. Like maybe she stayed up all night, tossing and turning and thinking about Jaws.

But instead of talking about that, she gripes, "Tell me again why we're bringing this bird to practice? Aren't we afraid she'll try to escape?"

"I told you, Gram. My teammates want to meet her, and it's easier to bring *her* to *them*. She can't escape with her tether on, but she might try to fly. I figure you never spend the whole practice on the actual sidelines. She can sit in the car with you in the air-conditioning when you get too hot."

What I *don't* add: *I need to bring Charlie to practice to make things right with Audrey and the others. They've been so upset with me lately. They're asking so many questions.*

As well they should. I mean, I'm investigating a murder and I owe money to a loan shark.

"We're running late," Grammy mutters as we get underway. She ignores the directions she's plugged into the GPS. "*RECALCULATING*," the device screams. "*RECALCULATING.*" We're zipping through the streets of Charleston, past pastel-colored houses and under wispy palm trees, when—

"Oh, crap!" Grammy says, and slams on the brakes.

Charlie wobbles on my knee and unfurls her wings to stay steady.

A horse-drawn carriage—the kind the tourists love—has pulled out right in front of us. The horse isn't fazed at all by our screeching brakes, but Grammy and I sit there panting.

I'm suddenly whisked away by a snapshot of Uncle Will piloting one of those things. I whip out my phone, wink at Grammy, and record the memory: "Uncle Will invited all of us—me, Grammy, Mom, Jacob, and

Uncle Frank—to ride in his carriage. He was so proud of that job—'You should see the tips!' he'd say. We all crammed in his tiny carriage, but his horse would *not* budge. 'C'mon, Cinnamon, please?' Will begged, but no. Finally, the horse lifted her tail and let loose the largest pile of dung you ever saw. It smelled so bad, our eyes watered, but then Cinnamon was ready. Our laughter mixed with the clip-clop-clip of Cinnamon's hooves the whole ride, while Jacob and Uncle Frank joked about Uncle Will's 'tips.'"

I turn the recorder off. Grammy smiles and her eyes glass over. "I'm glad you're recording those memories," she says. "You'll be happy you have those later."

I sniff. "I thought it would be easier by now," I whisper.

Grammy steers around the carriage—"*RECALCULATING!*" shouts the GPS—and she sighs. "Grief is unexpressed love for someone we've lost," she says. "I read that yesterday."

I have a lot of unexpressed love, I guess. "I sure wish I'd've expressed it."

"Me too."

Grammy sighs. "Grief doesn't just—poof!—disappear. We'll have Willie with us always. Sometime soon these memories will feel better. Lighter. Maybe even happy. But now . . . ?"

Grammy's voice gets tangled into what sounds like a knot in her throat. I know she's thinking about loan sharks and debts and stalkers and possible murder. We're way late now and the GPS won't stop harassing us about it.

Charlie senses the mood in the car. She claps her beak twice, shuffles her feet, and shouts, "RECALCULATING!"

The tears stinging my eyes turn into laughter, sliding down smiling cheeks. That's another thing grief is: a whole wad of emotions tangled together, like necklaces you love but can't wear because of the frustrating work required to untangle them.

Charlie is pleased she's made us laugh. "Ha-ha," she says. I love when she "imitates" human laughter like that. "RECALCULATING."

Grammy squints at Charlie from the corner of her eye, but she's grinning wide. "Hush, turkey."

Mom smiles and says, "There you are!" when we approach her on the sideline, but she scowls when she sees Charlie. Every one of my teammates squeals. Jumps. Claps. I grin.

"What does she eat?"

"How heavy is she?"

"Can I hold her?"

"Does she bite?"

"Does she poop on you?"

"Is that a tiny bird leash?"

"Why doesn't she fly away?"

Charlie ruffles her feathers, squawks, and claps her beak twice. She cocks her head at my teammates, then at the vast blue sky over the soccer pitch. It's like that last question gives her a plan. She spreads her wings, leaps—

—and sails down to the back of one of the canvas camp chairs sitting on the sideline. She grips it and sways.

My teammates coo and *ahhh* at her. Reach for her. I ask them to give her some room, and I scoop her up and give her to Grammy.

"Birds are skittish," I say. "They know they're small and light in this big, heavy world."

I look to each teammate in turn and start answering:

"She eats lots of stuff, but mainly corn. She loves corn."

"Not that heavy, but your arm can get tired keeping her propped up. It works better when she sits on my shoulder or on top of my head."

"It's not really good for a lot of folks to hold her. Birds get sick real easy. And their metabolism is wild! Her heart can beat six hundred times a minute, so illness travels fast in her system."

"Yes, she bites. Hard. It hurts."

"Yes, she poops on me. A lot."

"Yep, it's a tiny leash. She can move around a lot in it. I love this thing. It lets me take Charlie so many places."

"She doesn't fly away because her wings are clipped." I gently lift Charlie's wing and show my teammates the row of long feathers at the back of the wing. "When these feathers are clipped, a bird can't lift. It doesn't hurt the bird—it's like getting a haircut. It's smart to do for birds that live inside. Otherwise, they might fly into ceiling fans or mirrors or windows and really hurt themselves. These feathers grow back like hair, so they have to be trimmed pretty often to keep her safe."

What I DON'T say: I'm still not sure how I feel about all that—clipping her wings to keep her safe. I love Charlie and of course I want to keep her safe. But is keeping her grounded the best way to love her? I know she's a pet and can't just be "set free." She likely couldn't find food or water on her own. She'd be easy prey for other animals. This area isn't her natural environment. But there's some things I wonder, now that Charlie lives with us, about birds living inside. Is protection always love? Are we loving her or limiting her?

Coach blows his whistle. "Game time, girls!"

Charlie flaps her wings and imitates Coach's whistle, one long, pitch-perfect note. "Game on! Pretty bird! AWK!"

My teammates' eyes get big and soft and their knees buckle and they clasp their hands at their hearts and they say, "Awwwww!" I love Charlie so much.

How far do you go to protect something you love?

Maybe . . . if you're Uncle Will . . . you don't tell them how sick you really are.

Or? Maybe you don't tell them a bunch of bad guys are after you.

Jaws's threat clangs through my head like a siren: *This kind of debt is like DNA, see. It passes from one family member to the next. It's a disease, and it'll kill each of you.*

Maybe he pulled away, trying to protect us from threats like that.

Grammy and I ride most of the way home in silence. Grammy is ticked because she was on Charlie duty for the whole match, and there was pooping.

A lot of pooping.

And Charlie is worn out. She's worked her way into the Mustang's small back seat and tucked her head under her wing.

We're almost home when I see it . . .

"The yellow Prius!"

I point at the vehicle a few cars up from us. The light turns green, and the Prius zooms ahead.

"Grammy, chase it!"

She tries for a bit, but the Prius weaves in and out of traffic and zooms off, disappearing around a seafood truck.

"Grammy, keep up!" I shout.

Grammy licks her teeth. "No, ma'am. Nope. I'm all for adventure and for figuring out this mystery behind Will's death—"

She believes me!

"—but no *Fast and Furious*. Nuh-uh. I'll take my Vin Diesel while sitting on a couch with a dirty martini, thank you."

I sigh. "I've been thinking. Jaws was lying. The Prius *has* to be someone who works for her, right? Why else would they be at Shorty's?"

Grammy clicks her tongue and nods. "I think you're right."

A few days ago, when we first started this investigation, my heart would've soared to hear Grammy say *I think you're right*. But now being right feels like this big, ugly, cold shadow creeping over us, so massive it blocks out the sun. Like Jaws lifting out of the churning ocean behind us. Goose bumps prickle my skin.

32

A CARD PARTY

At home, I try to build the next layer of my painting of Uncle Will. I need to finish this soon so I can be that much closer to the prize money. I've blocked in the background and the rough shapes of the face, but now it's time to add details.

The hard stuff. The stuff that makes it *look* like Uncle Will.

Inhale, exhale.

Shiny little gems of paint line my palette. Something Ms. Umar told us in our last class echoes through my head: *A portrait, to be a work of art, may or may not resemble the person. One must paint its atmosphere.* She said she was paraphrasing an artist named Umberto Boccioni there.

My phone pings. It's Dad: **How was the match, kiddo? Passing with the left leg working better?**

Inhale, exhale.

I'll start with Uncle Will's nose. I might as well dive in with the hardest thing first. Noses are harder to paint than just about anything, even harder than painting hands.

Two hundred fifty dollars. My stomach squeezes.

I swipe on color. Ugh, too thick.

I sigh. Try to lift some of the paint off the canvas. It smears wider.

Charlie paces the footboard of my bed, flustering and flapping. Her toenails clicking on the wood sound like a ticking clock in my head, reminding me that both this painting and the money that Uncle Will owes are due in two days. She whistles and ducks her head under her wing. "Where's Will?" she whistles. "Wheeeeere's Will?"

I huff. "That is such a creepy question, Charlie. It freaks me out every time you do that."

My phone pings again. Dad: **I could get you some private lessons with a soccer coach here in Asheville this summer. What do you think?**

Focus, Chloe. Focus.

I'll fix the nose later. Let's move on to the eyebrows.

Eesh! Way too thick and dark. Uncle Will looks like a Neanderthal. My teeth grind.

Charlie claps her beak—*click-click-click*—and whistles a little ditty. She hops onto my bed, then back onto the footboard, then onto my bed, then back onto the footboard. She tucks her head under her wing, then peeks above it. "Where's Will? Where is he?"

Chills ripple over my skin. I shrug off the shiver. "You miss him, too, don't you, girl?"

Ping! Dad again: **I just know you'll be unstoppable if we can figure out that left foot.**

"We"? It's my stupid foot!

Breathe.

Inspiration. I need inspiration. I dig through the box of stuff that Uncle Will left to Uncle Frank, looking for ideas. I toss items onto the bed: a few Robin Hood T-shirts; a battered, dog-eared copy of Agatha Christie's *Cards on the Table*; and a necktie that has Mickey Mouse and Goofy golfing all over it. A memory snapshot: Uncle Will wore this tie to my preschool graduation.

More playing cards.

I slide the cards out of the box, fan them, and smell them. The rich, papery smell of playing cards makes me happy-sigh. I love the slick texture and how the cards glide like oil between your fingers. I dump them in a pile on my bedspread and smear them into a messy amoeba shape. Charlie hops around the pile, squawking and chirping like she's just found the perfect nest.

She flaps wildly. "Peekaboo! Here I am, Charlie! Peekaboo! Hey, Charlie!"

Tears sting my eyes. Oh, I see! Will used to play peekaboo with her. *That's* what that creepy "Where's Will?" question means!

I cover my eyes with my hands. "Where's Chloe? Where is she? Wheeeeere's Chloe?" But Charlie has moved on to playing with the cards.

I shake my head and turn back to the painting.

Eyes. I'll try his eyes.

But the moment I start painting them, I know they're too blue. Too wide. Too weird. I slam my paintbrush into the muddy water next to my canvas. I stare at the not-quite portrait of my favorite uncle.

Two hundred fifty dollars.

Charlie whistles and clicks. "Peekaboo! Here I am!" Normally, I love hearing her noisy bird chatter, but today it's setting my teeth on edge. Every part of me feels frustrated.

Should I even be painting Uncle Will? *This* is who I pick as my hero? This guy who kept all these secrets and owed all this money and pulled away from all of us at the end and, and . . .

My fists ball and I hiss-whisper to the portrait, "Why did you leave us this huge mess to figure out? Huh? Why are we cleaning up after you, *still*?" I'm shaking. "Why didn't tell us you were so sick? Why would you leave like this?"

I feel heat creeping up the back of my neck. Charlie marches through the pile of cards on the bed. "Awk! Good bird. Awk!" She whistles a two-note song and picks up a card in her beak. She rips it into bits and spits it on my carpet, then starts nibbling on the next card.

My jaw might turn to dust, I'm clenching it so hard. "No," I whisper, and it tastes like harsh lemon. "No. You didn't leave us this mess—you intended to clean it up, right? You *weren't* sick. You *didn't* know you were dying. Someone surprised you. Someone *hurt* you. . . ."

I pick up the sloshing wet paintbrush and slash it across the canvas. It makes a total mess of Uncle Will's face. Eyes and eyebrows and nose become a puddle.

"You were murdered! You would've told me if you were that sick. *You would've told me.*"

The canvas is a wet, muddy mess. Charlie must sense my anger because she hops onto the footboard again and tries to fly onto my shoulder.

But she misses, of course. She's a terrible flyer, thanks to those clipped wings. She whacks into the mess of a portrait on the easel. The easel crashes to the floor, and muddy water splashes everywhere. The canvas flies and lands—of course—paint-side down on my carpet. "No!"

Charlie, splotched with wet paint, flaps around on

the floor. I scoop her up. "Are you okay?" I place her on my desk and dab at her with paper towels. Her silvery gray feathers are dotted with peach and blue and brown paint. "Charlie? Are you hurt?" She blinks and cocks her head at me like she doesn't understand all this fuss. She's okay!

Charlie grabs the paper towel and nibbles it. "Pretty Charlie. I love you, Will."

Will!

I scoop up the canvas. It landed on the bits of ripped-up playing card Charlie spit on my floor. The confetti-like bits stick in the paint, dotting the portrait. Like a card party. Poker night.

"Charlie," I breathe. "It's perfect!"

I frantically rip up bits of blue playing cards and smoosh them into the thick, wet paint. Some bits are face up with the card symbols showing, some show the backs of the cards. Charlie has a ball helping me. She kicks up one foot, then the other, and bobs her body up and down. That's her happy dance, the one she does when she's giggling.

After I've ripped up about fifteen cards and attached them to the canvas, I step back. This collage—it's the perfect way to celebrate Uncle Will. Card confetti. It's truly building a painting, layering these cards in with the paint.

I look at the swirly blue back of one of the cards. "It's exactly his eye color, isn't it, Charlie?"

"Charlie girl!" Charlie squawks. "Pretty bird! Want a kiss?" She's still nibbling cards into bits for me. Still dancing.

Ping! I glance at my phone screen, expecting the text to be from Dad. Instead, it's Uncle Frank: **On my way to pay off Jaws. Just gonna get it over with today so we can stop worrying about it. Thought I should let y'all know.**

There's a pause—dot dot dot—and then another message: **In case something happens.**

Grammy immediately replies: **Come get us. We're going, too.**

Jacob: **yeah dude don't go alone**

As much as I don't want to go back to Shorty's and see that awful troll again, I smile. My family. We're in this together.

I gather up Charlie and glance at the mess of cards and paint littering my bedroom floor. This portrait—I'll finish it soon. But right now, I gotta go pay off a loan shark.

Go go go.

33

THE END OF MY ACTING CAREER

If this were a scene in the movies, the four of us (plus Charlie) would stride into Shorty's in slow motion. We'd form a wide line, shoulder to shoulder, and the soundtrack would be something bold, like "Seven Nation Army" by the White Stripes, and we'd narrow our eyes and toss our long manes of hair and walk in perfect sync to the drumbeat.

Instead, we pile out of Uncle Frank's fancy SUV like clowns from a clown car. Grammy smooths Uncle Frank's hair down like it's school picture day. He scowls and mutters, "Mom. Is this necessary?"

Grammy huffs. "It's always important to be presentable, yes."

Presentable. Both Uncle Frank and Grammy look

like zombies, pale, with purple-ringed eyes, like they haven't slept in a week. I wish I could stop this. Everything about this feels icky and wrong. How can I possibly stop it, though?

Jacob is so nervous, he starts doing knee-to-chest jumps like they do in football practice. Charlie, who always seems to have a read on the mood, cocks her head to and fro and claps her beak, like she's working kinks out of her neck. I snicker despite myself. That's what I do when I get nervous—I laugh. I can't help it. Once, in a third-grade production of *Schoolhouse Rock!*, I was supposed to be the singing bill on Capitol Hill. Instead, I was a giggling piece of paper on a stepladder, all while Ms. Johnson, the music teacher, scowled at me.

It was the end of my acting career.

Jaws offers us a seat in a booth inside the bar, but Grammy shakes her head. "This won't take long."

Jaws smirks and strokes her chin. "Suit yourself." Her grandson, the hulking bartender, looms nearby.

Oh no. I feel it coming on. Coming UP. The nervous giggles. And the harder you fight them, the worse they get.

Jaws narrows her eyes at us. "You're early. Not too many of my clients pay up early."

The absurdity of where we are right now makes my

shoulder twitch. And twitch again. Charlie bobs on my shoulder so much that she climbs atop my head. I hate that this troll of a woman is going to win, and yet somehow, I can't stop laughing. I can't stop *any* of this awfulness!

Jaws shifts her eyes to me, then back to Uncle Frank. "You're the one paying, I presume?"

Uncle Frank nods and pulls a piece of paper from his jacket pocket. "My car title. I'm going to sign it over to you. I assume that's okay?"

Jaws squints at him. "Make and model?"

Uncle Frank points out the smoky glass front door. His shiny tank of a car, a Cadillac SUV, is parked curbside. Jaws shrugs like it's not the most beautiful car ever. Uncle Frank whips out his sleek gold pen, rolls it between his fingers, and bends over a table to sign away his dream car.

"And you'll give us the name of the person in the yellow Prius?" Grammy adds.

Jaws smirks, nods, and waves her hand in a *get on with it already* motion.

It's not funny. My brain knows it's not funny, and yet I'm still twitching.

Another problem with absurdity is that it's contagious. Jacob feels my barely contained bursts of laughter lingering *just* under my skin, and he grins. Shakes his head. But it's no use. His shoulders start to shake, too.

Jaws scowls. She's used to people quaking in their boots before her, not holding in huge bouts of laughter. "Is something funny here, folks?"

Grammy snorts. Places her fingertips gently over her smile. "No. It's nothing . . . *Mildred*."

Three of us—minus Uncle Frank, who frowns deeply in our direction—crackle with held-in laughter. Charlie seems to be confused by the mixture of nervousness and giggling. She shifts on top of my head and says, "Ha-ha!" in that way that sounds like a person saying "ha-ha," not actual laughter. My shoulders shake so hard, a tear rattles out of the corner of my eye.

Uncle Frank touches the point of his pen to the car title, then stops. He sighs.

Jaws fumes red. She knows exactly how to stomp on an army of ants. "Well, it's about time these debts got paid. Will didn't know the first thing about money. I'm not surprised he couldn't manage his health. Guy couldn't even manage a debit card. He was a cheater, too, always bringing in those marked cards of his. A swindler!"

My insides churn from absurdity to anger, like the flip of a light switch. All that tension roils into rage. This woman, just shrugging off Uncle Will's debts! Uncle Will's *death*! It's one card too many on this house of cards.

"No!" I say too loudly, trying to hear myself over the sound of my heart pounding in my ears. I grab Uncle Frank's sleeve and lift the pen off the paper. "We're not paying you." I swipe my phone out of my pocket and wiggle it at Mildred and the bartender. It's still open to the voice recorder app from the last snapshot I recorded.

"I've recorded this whole conversation. And we'll go to the police if you don't stop doing this to people. We're not paying you."

"Call the police," Charlie squawks. She flaps her wings. "Call 911!"

Jaws turns pale. "What the—?"

I gulp past the lump in my throat and plow on. "And I bet the police would pay extra attention, since this *client* of yours is now dead." I said it—I said *dead*. "Young guy, now gone . . . ? Seems real suspicious, don't you think?"

"Suspicious!" Charlie crows. "It was murder!"

Jaws's jaw hangs open. She shakes her head, too fast. "That bird—that bird is a *liar*!"

Every muscle in this bar tightens, I can feel it. The hulking bartender takes a step toward me. Jacob and Uncle Frank step up to him.

Tension tastes and feels like the bile in your stomach creeping up your esophagus. But I don't break eye contact with Mildred. With *Jaws*.

Jaws looks like she's sucked on a lemon. "You don't

want the name of your stalker? In that Prius?"

I try not to show my hesitation. We can find out the driver of the yellow Prius on our own. We've made it this far, haven't we? Me and my family—we can do anything, as long as we do it together.

I wave my phone at her again. "We're *not paying*."

"Call the police!" Charlie is on a roll now. "It was murder!"

Mildred narrows her eyes. She purses her lips and turns to Grammy. "I'll forgive Will's loan."

Forgive the loan must mean she's dropping it, that we don't have to pay her back, because Grammy's and Uncle Frank's shoulders relax for the first time in days. Uncle Frank tucks the title to his car back inside his jacket.

Jaws's face hardens suddenly, and she snatches a butter knife out of the hand of a nearby customer. "But don't you tell a soul I did this, you hear?" She swivels to the rest of the bar, making it known that she means everyone here. "Any of you tell, or if that recording gets out—"

Her tight, wrinkled gaze scans us all and lands on Charlie. "You tell, and I come after that no-good, lying bird."

She jabs the rounded tip of the knife in Charlie's direction. From her perch on my shoulder, Charlie squawks, flutters her wings against my head, and poops on the bar's concrete floor.

Jaws—*Mildred*—looks like a gargoyle. Back hunched, eyes narrowed, teeth bared. I'm frozen in fear, the point of the knife inches from my face. Even though it's just a butter knife, she means this threat.

Jaws twiddles the knife between her fingers like a drumstick and offers the handle of it back to her customer. The guy gulps and takes it from her, placing it on the far end of the table.

Jaws inhales, softens, and becomes Mildred again. "Look at that. I'm nothing but a big old softie. Isn't that right, Rose?"

My grammy is forced to nod. "Yes, Mildred. Such a kind and forgiving heart."

Mildred nods, cracks her knuckles. "I think it's time for you to go." She storms off toward the kitchen.

Uncle Frank nods super fast. He takes his mother by the elbow. "I agree. Come on, family. . . ."

We're almost to the door, but Grammy just can't help herself. She mutters, "I still can't believe *Mildred* is a *loan shark*."

"Shark!" Charlie squawks. "Awk! Shark! Bay-bee SHARK dodododododo! Baby SHARK dodododododo!"

"WHAT DID THAT BIRD SAY?" Mildred screams from the kitchen.

We eye each other and *run*.

34

YOU CALLED A LOAN SHARK'S BLUFF

We tumble out the door and crash into Uncle Frank's SUV, then peel out of the parking lot like his tires are on fire. Uncle Frank drives to Riverfront Park, pulls into a space, and slams the car to a stop. We sit there in silence for a moment, panting, looking out over the light bouncing off the Cooper River. The sun turns the water into a sheet of diamonds.

Jacob flips the back of his hand against my arm. "Smart thinking, recording that convo, sis."

I gulp, and it's like swallowing a lump of sawdust. "Next time, remind me to actually *turn on the recorder*!"

Grammy spins to look at me from the front seat, her eyes wide. "That wasn't really recorded?"

Will my spit glands ever work again? My mouth is so dry! I shake my head. I guess my acting career *didn't* end with *Schoolhouse Rock*. "I thought of you grabbing that photo of the yellow Prius license plate the other day. And, well, I've been recording so many thoughts lately, so I . . . improvised."

Uncle Frank exhales long and low. "You called her bluff! Chloe, I can't believe you called a loan shark's bluff."

Grammy chuckles. "That woman is an expert in poker. She usually knows a bluff when she sees one."

Poker. Jaws said something about Uncle Will having marked cards . . . ?

Charlie nudges my cheek with the top of her fuzzy bird head, and I snap out of the thought.

I smile. "I learned from the best."

Grammy is the first to snort a laugh. Soon, we're all laughing and watching the seagulls attack a tourist who tried to feed one of them a Cheeto. And this time, the laughter doesn't turn rancid like sour milk. It doesn't flip into anger like a light switch. It just melts into smiles.

Jacob is the first one to say it. "So who's in that yellow Prius, you think?"

Uncle Frank and Grammy shake their heads at the same time, same pace. You can see, at moments like this, the mother-son resemblance.

"Obviously someone who knew Will well," Uncle Frank says. "He's in all the same places we are."

The silence speaks loudly: maybe someone who knew Will even better than we did.

Charlie watches the seagulls, those long-lost cousins of hers, dipping and lifting with such ease. She blinks and cocks her head at them, ducking to get a better view out of the car window. They fly. They flock. My heart knows why she's staring.

We all just want to find our flock and fly.

On the drive home, I lean my forehead against the cool glass, thinking about mysterious Priuses and loan sharks and marked cards. Just because Jaws isn't making us pay Will's debts doesn't mean she's innocent. She could definitely be involved with his death. She's a menace, and still absolutely, positively a suspect. The way she threatened Charlie? It's like Charlie knows something we don't.

Charlie nudges me with her head. "Dessert spoon! Not soup spoon, knucklehead!"

Grammy turns in her seat to squint at Charlie. "That bird."

Uncle Frank chuckles. "That bird."

35

Back in my room, I study the swirly blue design of the cards that are still scattered all over the place. I tilt a card in the slant of the setting sun from my bedroom window, and I confirm: yep, there is a depression in the waxy card. Someone has written a tiny letter *M* on the back of the blue card in blue ballpoint pen.

I snatch up a handful of other cards. "Hey!" Charlie shouts at me. "Pretty girl!"

Yep. These cards—they're all marked. A letter *F*. A letter *W*. An *S* . . .

Jaws was right. Marked cards. That's what some poker players do to cheat. They use marked cards to read what the other players are holding.

A feeling is rising inside me like an ocean tide—this

means something. I squint harder at the cards. I swirl them under my fingertips like someone might stir the surface of a puddle. "What do these letters mean?" I whisper. I look up at the portrait of Uncle Will. The canvas is still quite a mess. "What does this mean?"

I always knew Uncle Will took some liberties with the rules. Pushed some boundaries. But cheating?

The letters hidden in the swirls of the cards make no sense. I try putting them in alphabetical order: ADFILMNORSUWY.

"Adfilminorsuwy." I stumble over the awkward letters, trying to read them. I glance at Charlie. "That mean anything to you?" Charlie is clutching a saltine and doesn't even look up.

"'Film' is in there. Like *Robin Hood*, maybe?" I flip to the page in my notebook where I've been recording all my password attempts. "But I've already tried that." Frustration buzzes inside me like a pesky mosquito.

"This is stupid," I say. "It probably doesn't mean anything other than Uncle Will was a cheater." That hurt more than I expected it to, saying that, even just to Charlie. I watch Charlie nibble her cracker for a bit. "Hey, Charlie!" I say, and when she looks my way, I cover my eyes. "Where's Chloe? Wheeeeere's Chloe? Where is she?"

Charlie spins, poops, and ignores me. My frustration buzzes louder. A swarm of stinging bugs.

I start sorting the cards by suit—all the clubs together, all the hearts together. There are duplicates, I notice—a couple of *F*s, three *Y*s . . . but each in a different suit. I look up at my mess of a painting.

"Why'd you have to cheat, huh? Why'd you leave us with nothing more than your mysterious death and this stupid alphabet soup of cards?" I growl—actually growl!—and swirl my hands through the neatly sorted piles. I'm left with a blue puddle of cards on the carpet. They swim under my tears.

I flip the cards between my fingers. A three of hearts. A jack of diamonds. A queen of spades. . . .

On an impulse, I put the cards in numerical order, starting at 2 and ending with ace. (All poker players know ace is high.) Then I flip each of the cards over. And the letters wake up, like they've been hiding in swirls of smoke or steam:

FAMILYSWONDRU

Family is wondrous. Each letter represents the number on the opposite side: 2 = F, 3 = A, 4 = M, and so on. Marked cards don't repeat letters within the suit, so the second letter *I*, the second *O*, and the second *S* were all omitted.

"Family is wondrous," I say aloud.

Charlie drops her saltine and cocks her head like she understands. "Awk! Family is wondrous!" She whistles, like she's highlighting the words I just spoke.

The moment she repeats it, I remember: *family is wondrous* is what Will said in his last will and testament video! The memory of the video rushes back like a very clear, very recent snapshot: *Family is wondrous*, he said. *That's all you need to know.*

"Family is wondrous!" I shout. I lunge to my desk, where Will's laptop is plugged in. "Family is wondrous!"

"What's all the hubbub?" Mom shouts. I hear her footsteps on the stairs.

I furiously type in *Family is wondrous*.

Nope.

Mom's footsteps get closer. I don't want her to catch me trying to break into Uncle Will's computer. She'd ask too many questions.

familyiswondrous—no spaces, no caps.

Nope.

"Chloe, is everything okay?" Mom walks down the hall.

One more shot. I type *FAMILYSWONDRU*—just like the cards are marked.

The screen flickers. The laptop makes that Windows sound, like a long, sighing, musical exhale.

I'M IN!

Mom rounds the corner into my doorway, and I slam the laptop closed. She probably wouldn't suspect anything weird—like, say, a murder investigation—if she found out I now know how to log in to Will's computer. But she likely *would* take the laptop from me to poke around in his accounts if she knew how to get in. I can't have her take the laptop now!

I smile at her. Her arms are crossed, and she's leaning against my doorframe, one eyebrow raised.

I point to the easel where my messy painting of Uncle Will stands.

"I, uh, had a breakthrough with the portrait," I stumble. "The cards. Don't you think they look good like that?"

Mom smiles. She loves art; she studied art history in college. Now she sells insurance.

"It does! Nice touch, sweetie."

She crosses to me, and I say a quick prayer that the heat of the laptop and the humming of its fan don't give me away.

She folds back my bangs and kisses my forehead. "My talented girl. Thanks for getting your chores done." Then she actually reaches over and scritches Charlie behind the ear. Or, well, where an ear would be, if birds had actual ears and not just hearing membranes.

Charlie whistles a two-note *thank you!*

Mom leaves, but the smell of her lavender lotion stays.

I smile after her and whisper, "Family is wondrous."

36

WHAT GRIEF FEELS LIKE

I decided to wait for the rest of my team before diving too deeply into Uncle Will's laptop—maybe I'm afraid of what I might find? Now Grammy and Jacob are huddled behind me in my room, door closed. Uncle Frank is on FaceTime. I type in the password, *FAMILYSWONDRU*, and Uncle Will's computer flickers to life.

"Yes!" Uncle Frank says. "Nice work, Chloe!"

Is it possible for a heart to smile? I think mine is grinning right now.

"Family is wondrous," Grammy repeats, twisting her necklace wistfully. "It sounds like something straight out of a Robin Hood movie. Like it has a sprinkle of magic over it."

My heart smile grows bigger.

"Start with his email," Uncle Frank says.

Grammy nods. "There's always evidence in the email. They talk about it all the time on *WHODUNNIT*. He might even have a secret email address we don't know about. We'll need to check for evidence of that, too."

Jacob points his thumb at Grammy. "Detective Grandma over here with her knowledge of crimes in rental cars and fake email addresses."

Grammy snuffs and holds up the palm of her hand. "Don't get me started about burner phones. We haven't even *looked* for one of those."

I suppress a grin at the thought of Uncle Will having a burner phone. He hated the small flip phone he had, and he barely kept it charged. He only agreed to carry it because Uncle Frank insisted he needed it for emergencies.

I read aloud the subject lines of the emails in Uncle Will's inbox: "Fifteen percent off House of Cards magic shop. Top Five Ireland destinations. Inspiring Quotes from Famous Buddhists. Fifty dollars in free chips at Grand Island Casino. Ooh! Twenty percent off sale at Dillard's this weekend."

Everyone chuckles. Charlie says, "Ha-ha," her odd

fake snicker, which makes everyone laugh more.

I scan the long list of unanswered email: "An overdue bill notice from South Broad Electric. An overdue bill from Citibank credit card. A notice from Charleston Gas that his account is in arrears."

"In a rear?" Jacob says, chuckling and elbowing Grammy. "Huhuh!" She shakes her head sternly and licks her teeth. I'm not exactly sure what *in arrears* means, but it doesn't sound good. My heart smile fades.

"Here's an email from Dr. Wallace: 'William Calhoun: you need to come in for further testing.'" A coldness creeps over us, like a gray cloud sliding over the sun. I keep reading.

"And another, from a Dr. Patel: 'We've tried calling you, Will, but your voice mail is full. Call us right away for your test results.'"

It almost feels like it's thundering here in my room. A hollow, creepy rumble, growing slowly louder as it approaches. Lighting always strikes next.

And another, from Dr. Kim: "You missed your last appointment, Will. Call us ASAP to reschedule. Your condition will not change without treatment."

Zap! There it is. The bolt of lightning.

Grammy blinks rapidly, stands abruptly. She heads for the door.

"Wait!" I say. "Where are you going?"

"Chloe," Grammy starts, then clears her throat. "Dear, it's over."

"No!" I look to Jacob, who studies the toes of his Converse. "No, I—"

Uncle Frank chimes in through FaceTime. "Chloe, I agree. What happened to Will was tragic, but it wasn't . . ."

His voice trails off. He can't even look at the camera. He can't say it. *Murder.*

"No!" I repeat. I feel frantic. "You can't quit now! You guys—we've made it so far! Look at the facts! We still have suspects, and Charlie knows all these weird words . . ."

"Fold your napkin!" Charlie chimes in. *Now* she chooses manners over murder? GAH!

"We're so close. Don't quit now." I know begging is uncool, but here I am. Begging.

Grammy crosses back to me and hugs me to her chest. She kisses me on my head, then releases me. "I love you, Bug. But no. No, Chloe. I'm sorry. Investigation over."

She leaves the room, bringing her phone with Uncle Frank's face on it. Jacob's eyebrows knit together. He shakes his head, claps me on the shoulder, and follows Grammy.

Charlie snaps her beak like she's biting back at this

terrible shift in our mood.

So many overdue bills. So many missed doctor appointments.

Did Uncle Will just . . . give up?

Should I?

I pace the stained fuzzy peach carpet in my room. Charlie paces the footboard of the bed, imitating me. I walk and spin, she walks and spins. And back again.

My pacing brings back a memory, this time of my dad's house. One summer when I was visiting my dad in Asheville, I broke a piece of his pottery. A coffee mug. He was cool with it—my dad rarely gets angry about anything but sports—but for weeks after, we'd find tiny, jagged shards hiding somewhere. In the shadows under a cabinet. Buried in the rug by the sink. Tucked in the corner next to the garbage can. And every once in a while, one of us would step on the tiniest sliver of pottery with bare feet. The shards were so small, you wouldn't even really bleed. You couldn't see them. You'd just have this awful stinging spot in your heel, with every step you took. For weeks, this happened—fine one minute, pain every step the next.

That's what grief feels like.

Was Uncle Will really just sick? Should I drop this whole investigation?

"This can't be right!" I turn to my half-finished portrait of Uncle Will. Will-in-progress. His face is a blur. I never want his face to be a blur.

"He was so *good*! He loved life! Why HIM? I don't understand a universe where a guy like Will has to die, and people like that awful Jaws woman get to keep running around, being terrible and lying and cheating and taking advantage of people. It's not *FAIR*!"

I grab more playing cards off my floor and tear them up furiously. Heat crawls up the back of my neck and I crumple the cards, then fling them to my carpet. "ARRRGH!" I whip toward Charlie. "He couldn't have been sick, right? He would've fought harder. If he knew he was dying, *he would've said goodbye!*"

Where is Uncle Will now? Like, not his body. We leave that behind. Our church says a lot about life after death, and I've been thinking about that lately. I do believe in heaven, but I still have so many questions. How can it be that the soul is in a body one minute and not the next? His body is still here, but where did *he* go? How does that *work*?

I stretch and curl my fingers. I pace. Charlie imitates me: She stretches and curls her claws. She paces. I grit my teeth. She claps her beak. Tears sting my eyes. Feathers ruffle on Charlie's back. She has bald patches where she's plucked too many feathers from stress.

She misses Uncle Will, too.

My throat clenches.

"If he was so perfect, why didn't he say goodbye?"

That's it, I realize. That's why I can't give up this stupid investigation. If Uncle Will knew he was going to die, he would've said goodbye to me. *That's* why I have to believe he was hurt instead.

I put my forehead gently against Charlie's forehead. We stand like that for a long while. Her head is a soft spot on mine, a small, warm pulse. Her heartbeat.

"Why didn't he say goodbye?" I whisper.

37

NOT YET

Uncle Frank shows up an hour later with a bucket of fried chicken and a watermelon.

"Well, well, look at you!" Mom says when she swings open the door. "To what do we owe this honor?"

Uncle Frank looks older than he did at the will reading, just a couple of weeks ago. He attempts a smile and shrugs. "Dunno. Thought you could use dinner? I wanted to see y'all."

"I will never turn down a dinner I don't have to cook," Mom says, and pulls him inside.

Mom goes into mom mode, microwaving a tub of mashed potatoes and slicing the watermelon and pulling out paper plates. We eat outside on the patio. The sun is setting, and the frogs are chirping, and the world smells like honeysuckle. It's weird how a day can be like a ride on a rope swing: so low one minute, you scrape your toes in the dirt; so high the next, your stomach flutters with joy.

While we eat, we hear Friendly and Charlie inside, through the screen of the sliding glass door. Friendly chatters at Charlie, who is high up on a perch inside his cage. Friendly makes the noise that cats only make for birds: *cickcickcickcick!* I can see her tail puff and twitch from out here.

"Friendlyyy . . . ," I warn.

But Charlie doesn't need my help. She shifts her bird belly, cocks her head at Friendly, and meows. "Rrroww!" It sounds just like Friendly.

Friendly is so confused, she arches her back, springs off the ottoman, and dives under the couch. We laugh. The trees wave in the warm breeze, and the long shadows of palm fronds dancing across the low, pink sun look like laughter, too.

It's a good dinner. We talk about school and sports. We don't talk about Uncle Will. I wonder when it won't hurt to talk about him.

"Help me clean up," Mom says, and nudges Jacob with her elbow. She heads inside with a stack of greasy paper plates. After a couple of trips back and forth,

Grammy motions for me, Jacob, and Uncle Frank to gather round outside. "Let's play cornhole!" she shouts too loudly. Way to be subtle, Gram. Jeez.

Mom appears next to the grainy metal screen door. "Cornhole? You? Really?"

Grammy juts her chin in the air. "They're starting a league at the senior center." Mom shrugs and ducks farther into the house, into the kitchen.

Jacob, Grammy, Uncle Frank, and I huddle on the patio. Grammy's hands shake as she whispers, "Chloe, I told you already that it's over—I can't help you with this investigation anymore. But I think you need to drop it, too. I just worry . . ." She pauses there. "I just worry."

"What? No!" I say, shaking my head. "We still have two suspects: Jaws, and the driver of the yellow Prius. And Jaws seems iffy. I'm not quitting now."

"I'm off the list?" Uncle Frank beams, and it's like watching him reverse-age in seconds. "I thought maybe I was, but I wasn't sure. Thanks, kiddo." He nudges me with his shoulder.

"You've proven your loyalty." I chuckle because it sounds like something I imagine Jaws would say.

"What are y'all whispering about?"

I jump. Mom leans against the wide silver frame of the screen door.

"Mother's Day is coming up," Grammy singsongs, like we're planning some big gift just for Mom. "Don't you go asking about secrets."

"Since when do you plan anything for Mother's Day?" Mom says, half her face pulled into a smirk. She eyeballs each of us, in that way only moms can. Like the conversation we were just whispering is etched into the air above us, and she's squinting, trying to read it.

"Why aren't you playing cornhole?" she asks.

Grammy doesn't like being questioned like this. "We're still choosing teams, Teresa."

"It takes that long to divvy up four of you?"

"Yes. It does."

Mom cocks her head, and it reminds me of Charlie. "You four have been spending quite a lot of time together lately." It's not a question, but . . . it is?

Uncle Frank clears his throat. "I've realized recently that, well, I want to be around you guys more." He doesn't say *since Will died*, but it's right there, the feeling of it.

"Without me?" Mom says. I can't tell if she's angry or upset.

"With you, Teresa!" Grammy interjects. "You're here now, yes?"

The moment is thick like the humidity out here has suddenly worsened. That's the feeling of the air right before a storm. Jacob sucks in a deep breath.

"Mom! I signed you up as Snack Parent for football tomorrow."

Mom's mood shifts from sad and confused to frustrated. "What?"

"You're Snack Parent! I forgot to tell you. I need to bring three dozen oranges to practice tomorrow."

Mom huffs a sigh and crosses her arms. "Tomorrow, Jake? And you're telling me *now*? At"—she looks at her watch—"eight p.m.? You can go get them, then."

Jacob does his puppy-dog-eyes thing, the thing that only works on Mom. He shrugs. "I guess I can. I'll just blow off studying for that big biology test . . ."

"Argh! Jacob Calhoun Alvarez!" Mom slams into the house. We hear her hand fishing through the key bowl. "I'll go," she shouts through the screen door. "Jacob, you study. The rest of you . . ." She points at me, Grammy, and Uncle Frank. "Finish cleaning this mess."

From the patio, we hear Mom slam the front door, muttering about how far away she's parked. The four of us stand there in silence.

"She knows," Grammy says.

Uncle Frank shakes his head. "She suspects. But she doesn't know." He lifts his chin at Jacob. "Good thing you remembered those oranges, dude. She was sniffing us out. That woman is a bloodhound."

Jacob shrugs. "I don't need to bring oranges tomorrow."

I blink. "What?"

"Mom was asking too many questions. I had to get her off our backs."

I inhale sharply. All of this is starting to feel super icky. I don't like the idea of shutting Mom out. Avoiding her was okay. Not great, but okay. But I don't like lying to her. Maybe if we explain the suspects list . . .

Grammy strides to the screen door and pauses. "Chloe. Dear. It's not that Will getting hurt by someone isn't a possibility . . ."

Her voice catches, but after a moment she finds it. "I've been thinking about all those emails. It sure does seem like Will was *sick* and not *hurt*." Uncle Frank nods. He offers Grammy the corner of a silk hankie from his pocket. She pulls and pulls—it's a magician's rainbow handkerchief, and Grammy is *not* in the mood. She huffs and tosses the puff of fabric back at Uncle Frank. Jacob drops into a camp chair and stares at the toes of his Converse.

I'm losing them! My teammates, my fellow detectives, walking away one by one. It took me so long to convince them, and now I'm losing them. I'm getting desperate here.

Grammy slides open the screen door, and it moans. Just as I feel our team bursting apart like a fragile soap bubble, Jacob leaps to his feet.

"The yellow Prius!"

We follow the direction of his pointing finger.

There it is, zipping up our street.

Me, Jacob, and Uncle Frank give chase.

We dash through five or six yards before we run out of breath. We stand there panting, hands on knees.

I shake my head. "Don't give up yet," I pant, and lift my chin in the direction the Prius went. "There's too much evidence."

Jacob nods. "Okay. Not yet."

Uncle Frank puts a fist against his chest. I worry he might be having a heart attack or something because he's an old person. "Okay, Chloe." He swallows. "Me too. Not yet."

The way they say it, though. It's like pity more than support. I can tell I have to start making headway on this mystery, and *fast*.

38

CAN YOU SPY ON A DEAD MAN?

With only one day left to work, I paint frantically. This portrait is due tomorrow, and boy, do I feel the pressure. Although now that Uncle Will's debts to Jaws are gone, I don't feel like I *have* to win. I *want* to.

"Carpe diem, carpe diem, carpe diem," I chant, trying to muster a whole day's worth of seconds under each brushstroke. All this stuff added to my plate lately has not made me happier, like I thought it would. Cramming more into a day hasn't been all that great. I try to imagine Uncle Will's portrait hanging in the Gibbes Museum downtown as part of the all-district art fair. Uncle Will believes in *manifesting* things—believing in them so wholeheartedly, you make them happen. Kinda like an answered prayer.

Believed. He *believed* in manifesting.

I wonder when I'll stop doing that.

The paint needs to dry, so *snip!*—I turn to trimming the playing cards with toenail clippers, trying to get the perfect curve for the irises of Uncle Will's eyes. Charlie is having a ball with all the bits of card flying everywhere. I laugh as she hops around on my desk, chasing the next morsel of card.

"Awk! Homicide! Call 911! Want a cookie?" Charlie squawks suddenly. That bird's deadly vocabulary will never not be creepy.

"What do you *know*?" I squint at her, but the bird's not spilling the beans.

I used to not say things like *spilling the beans*. This mystery has changed me.

I sigh and open Uncle Will's laptop. Maybe I missed something. Maybe . . .

I return to his email, where Grammy and Uncle Frank are convinced there will be evidence. But who puts their intent to hurt someone in an email? I imagine it:

To: Will

From: Jaws

Subject: Murdering You

I shrug and open his inbox anyway.

I scroll twice, three times. Hmm. What about his

sent emails? Outgoing instead of incoming. When I click that folder, I laugh.

Uncle Will only sent like four emails this year. Even I know that's not a lot. He was an old person—Gen X is all about the email.

But one email in particular catches my eye.

I click it.

Dear Mr. Josh Adams of Adams Literary, it begins. *I am seeking representation for my 75,000-word young adult manuscript . . .*

Wait. What?! My eyes scan the rest of the message.

Manuscript?!

I frantically click over to Microsoft Word. (That's how you know *for sure* he was Gen X—that Microsoft loyalty.) I click on File, then Open Recent. There's a list of the last documents Uncle Will opened and worked on. It's a bit creepy, doing this. It feels like spying.

Can you spy on a dead man?

The top document is called "Will's Will." His last will and testament. It's a rough outline of what he said in his video in that smelly lawyer's office.

But the next document.

The title reads "It's Bad Manners to Murder Your Etiquette Teacher."

I click it, and Word whirls it open. I scan the first page. It appears to be a title page: the name of the story,

Will's full name, the word count. And the subtitle: "A Young Adult Murder Mystery."

I gulp. Scroll to page two.

And there. On page two. My eyes immediately swim with tears. Because the page two dedication reads:

For Chloe, my fellow family artist

"Mom!" I shout when I finally find my voice. "MOM!"

Charlie echoes me: "Mom!"

Mom yells up the stairs. "What?"

"C'mere!" I yell. "You're going to want to see this!"

Mom strolls oh-so-casually into my room. "Heavens, Chloe! What is—oh! Is everything okay?"

Tears stream down my cheeks, cool lines on my hot face. But I nod. I point to Uncle Will's laptop. "Read this."

"Mom!" Charlie shouts again.

Mom leans over my shoulder and begins reading aloud:

"'It's Bad Manners to Murder Your Etiquette Teacher'—ha! Oh my goodness..."

"What?"

Mom scrolls farther into the manuscript and continues reading aloud:

"'It was a bright and sunny day. A cheery day. A wondrous day—'"

I smile. Wondrous.

"'It was the exact opposite of the kind of day where you'd expect to stumble over a dead body.'"

Charlie suddenly sits erect on my desk and cocks her head. "A wondrous day!" she cackles. "Dead body!"

I blink.

Mom keeps reading: "'I should've called the police, of course. But I couldn't do that. I knew if I did, I'd be . . .'"

Charlie chimes in at this point, mirroring exactly what Mom reads: "THE NUMBER ONE SUSPECT IN A MURDER."

Charlie adds an *awk!* at the end, like an exclamation point.

Mom reads, "It's a homicide." Charlie repeats it.

Mom reads, "Call 911!" Charlie repeats it.

Mom reads, "Not for nothing, but Mrs. Cherry was a terrible old biddy . . ."

And Charlie finishes the line: ". . . and I'm glad she's dead! AWK!"

Mom looks up from the screen. "It's . . . a tongue-in-cheek murder mystery."

"Tongue-in-cheek?"

"A spoof. Satire. Like *Saturday Night Live*. And . . ." Mom scrolls farther and farther on the screen. "It's a whole novel."

I have a snapshot flash of Uncle Will pointing to a huge maple tree in Hampton Park. It was the same day my dad told us he was moving to Asheville. I was crying. Uncle Will flung an arm over my shoulder, and in that moment, I knew without him saying: anything I'd needed from my dad, *here*, Uncle Will would now do, no questions asked. *Look right there—a white squirrel! White squirrels, Chlo—they're really rare! They're good luck! Make a wish! Remember this moment! Woo-hoo, jackpot! We're gonna have a good life!*

My feelings right now are just like they were at that white-squirrel moment: that rare instant when you truly laugh and you truly cry at the same time. An emotion explosion. Relief and joy and sadness and grief all spill out.

Mom strokes my back. "Honey—are you okay?"

Am I okay? I . . . yes! I am better than okay!

Charlie is repeating the words of Uncle Will's murder mystery! Uncle Will obviously read it aloud so many times, Charlie learned the words.

That's how Charlie knows words like *homicide* and *skull* and *murder*!

The truth was always right there, but I didn't want to see it. Maybe if things with Uncle Will had ended with us as one big happy family, I would've believed the truth. But I couldn't, because I was just too hurt.

Uncle Will wasn't killed.

Uncle Will was sick.

Very sick.

So sick, he hid from us as he died.

And as sad as I am about that, I now know: He wasn't hurt or scared by someone else. He left Earth like he wanted to. His choices were imperfect, but they were his.

Relief settles over me like I had been hauling around a backpack full of bricks, and now I get to set that backpack down. Will wasn't perfect, but he loved harder than anyone I know, and that counts for a lot. "Uncle Will wrote a book! And he dedicated it to me."

That day in the library, during my After School Service, I had asked the stained ceiling if I was on the right track. I wrapped tiny magnifying glass stickers around mystery novels, and I knew in my gut that I was close to an answer. And funny enough, I had been! Closer than I even knew.

Mom smiles and turns to my portrait of Uncle Will, perched on my easel. And I see now: The painting is done. It's ready. I'd thought earlier that I wanted to paint like I was copying the world, that my image should be neat and tidy and exact. But this painting! It's loud and colorful and exuberant and happy and messy. Just like Uncle Will.

Mom wraps me up in a huge hug and kisses the top of my head. We stay like that a long time. It feels like the most perfect place, like where all the paints blend and layer smoothly.

Still wrapped in that warm hug, Mom says, "'If you want the rainbow, you gotta put up with the rain.' Or something like that. We've had a lot of rain lately. It's about time for our rainbow."

I nod. "Dolly Parton."

Mom pulls back a bit and looks me in the eyes. "Yes! How did you know that?"

My heart skitters. I shrug out of the hug. We're quiet for a minute, but then I can't help asking: "Mom, do you believe in psychics?"

Mom blinks. "Hmm. I'm not sure. Why do you ask?"

"Grammy's WHODUNNIT podcast. They used a psychic to help solve a cold case. It was wild." It's not a lie—there was an episode all about this, and it *was* wild.

Mom shrugs. "Whatever gives people comfort is a good thing, right? Doesn't really matter if I believe it or not. Sometimes people just need relief from all the stuff rattling around in their brain. That might look like a therapist or a preacher or a psychic—whatever helps."

She suddenly bursts out laughing. Her eyes shine

when she looks at the portrait again. Mom *never* cries, not even at Uncle Will's memorial service, so this is kinda monumental. She taps the corner of his laptop.

"Will, you amazing son of a biscuit-eater. This is one a heck of a last act, brother."

39

FAMILY MEETING, ASAP

Mom texts our family group chat, something that hasn't happened since Uncle Will was alive. His number is still on there; no one wants to remove it. Mom closed his Verizon account a couple of weeks ago; I wonder if someone else now gets her urgent message:

Family meeting ASAP. Our living room.

Twenty minutes later, the gang's all here. Mom paces the floor, balancing Uncle Will's laptop on the palms of her hands. Uncle Frank raises an eyebrow at me, and I can hear the question it's asking: *Are we busted?* I smile and shake my head.

Mom clears her throat and begins reading. No introduction, nothing. Just jumps right into Uncle

Will's story about the murder of a woman who teaches etiquette lessons out of her fancy home. It's a story about a summer class to teach teens good manners: Folding napkins properly. Using the correct fork. How to eat an artichoke in "polite company." The teacher—Mrs. Cherry—was so judgmental, it was no surprise she wound up dead. Poisoned with cyanide. It's a riveting murder mystery. And in it, the main character pulls further and further away from his family as suspicions point toward him. He's trying to protect them, he rationalizes. But the character feels regret about that, the pulling away. Deep regret.

I feel that part in the pit of my stomach, like a punch.

Charlie climbs up and down the walls of her cage behind Mom, chiming in at parts and ad-libbing others:

"Open an investigation! AWK!"

"Rule out accidental death. Who's a pretty bird?"

"Call in a lineup of suspects! Charlie want a cracker?"

The words of the story sound just like Uncle Will telling one of his wild college tales. And Charlie's repeats are so droll; she says "murder" in the same flat, uninterested way she says "ha-ha" when we laugh. The air in the room sparkles with joy for the first time in months.

After about five chapters, my mom pauses. "Mom,

are you okay?" We all turn to Grammy, whose face is buried in a pillow. Her shoulders shake.

Yikes!

Maybe hearing Uncle Will's words intertwined with so much talk about death and dying was too much for her? Uncle Frank lays a gentle hand on her back.

Grammy lifts her face out of the pillow and sucks in a huge breath. She's . . . laughing? Tears stream down her face, but yes. She's definitely howling with laughter.

"I guess Willie didn't like all those etiquette classes I made him take when he was fifteen!" she pants through her laughter. "The teacher was even named Mrs. Cherry!"

Mom and Uncle Frank laugh, too. "Mrs. Cherry's Charm School. Those classes were awful," Uncle Frank says with a chuckle. "It's a terrible thing to do to teens in the summer, Mom. The last class was a *formal ball*. Tuxes, in Charleston, in July? Ugh. So much sweat. *Teenage* sweat. While learning how to waltz."

"Dude, that sounds miserable," Jacob says.

"It was."

Mom smiles with her whole self. "Will used to call Mrs. Cherry 'Coach.' 'Hey, Coach Cherry! What kind of manners are we learnin' 'bout today?' Oh, she'd get so angry with him!"

They're all three laughing now, and Jacob and I

smile at each other behind their backs. This is nice. This is how it used to be. How it's supposed to be.

The way Grammy looks right now reminds me of a silver party balloon: once flying high and fully buoyant, but now a little deflated. Still fighting for height, though. Still floating, long after the good memories have been made.

"I called the specialist Will was seeing. Dr. Kim?" Her hands fidget. "She was very nice. Filled in a lot of blanks for me. Willie did exactly what he wrote, like his character. He pulled away from us because he thought he could protect us. The doctor, she said that happens quite a bit.

"She reminded me that people die how they live. Willie lived *big*, didn't he? Full of curiosity and wonder, questioning *everything*." Grammy snorts a laugh through her tears. "So of course he'd leave us the same way."

"Ms. Umar said that art is a denial of death." I squeeze Grammy's hand. "That's what Uncle Will did with this book. His curiosity and questions and wonder? They live on in this story." Grammy squeezes my hand back and nods.

Uncle Frank takes a deep, sharp breath. "I think we need to get that book published. I'll reach out to Mr. Adams and see what he thought."

Mom nods and looks at her big brother's words on a computer screen. "I'll research the process. I have no idea how to publish a book. Guess we'll find out."

Five bowls of ice cream later (six, if you count that Jacob had seconds), we finally tell Mom about our murder theory. She glowers at Uncle Frank and Grammy for going along with it, but then she laughs and tousles my hair.

"Let me get this straight: You invented a murder mystery about Uncle Will, and the mystery was that he'd invented a murder mystery about someone else?"

There is a pause before we all burst with laughter. "Yep," Jacob says. "That's pretty much it."

We laugh about our mystery for a bit longer, and then I gather up my courage like Charlie plucks up tufts of her feathers. "Mom?"

"Yes, Chlo?"

"What happened between you and Will? Like, you two used to spend so much time together. And then, you didn't. You know—even *before* he got sick. Before he pulled back from us all."

Mom runs her finger through the chocolate sauce in the bottom of her bowl and licks it off. Jacob arches an eyebrow at me—Mom *never* does stuff like that. Too germy.

She finally answers: "Well, time. Life. Too many things going on, and not enough time to do it all."

She pauses and continues: "It was also a bunch of little things, like Will always saying 'Carpe diem!' And that *Robin Hood* quote he loved: 'Rise and rise again, until lambs become lions.' Will was always telling me to lighten up, and I was always telling him to grow up. We just drifted apart."

She pauses a moment, and her voice wavers over the next part: "You think you'll have time to repair those fractures. Sometimes you don't."

It's quiet a minute longer, and then she reaches over and grabs Uncle Frank's hand. She points between me and Jacob with her free hand. "You two stick together, *always*. Got it?"

"Got it," I say. I smile at Jacob. He puts me in a headlock and rubs his knuckles across my scalp.

"Oh, she will NEVER GET RID OF ME, MOM," he says. "Right, Squeak?"

Jerk.

But he's *my* jerk. I poke him in the ribs, right where I know he's so ticklish he can't stand it.

Uncle Frank winks at Mom. "Headlock?"

"Don't you dare."

40

GRIEF TAKES TIME. SO DOES PAINTING.

"Mom, I'm taking your car to drive Chloe to school!" Mom shouts to Grammy in the rear of the house. We're late, and Grammy's car is right there in the driveway rather than half a mile up the street.

"Okay, dear," Grammy yells. I can hear the breathiness in her voice; she's sneaking another cigarette in the bathroom.

Mom's driving me to school because I'm bringing in Uncle Will's portrait today. It's bulky and lumpy, and *maybe* still a little sticky-wet, so I'm sitting in the back seat with it. When I buckle it into the seat next to me, it makes me fully laugh. It's Uncle Will in his Hawaiian shirt, a pirate hat, and an eye patch. Charlie perches on his shoulder, her head cocked. He's beaming with laughter, and bits of playing cards make up the flowers in his shirt and the twinkle in his eyes.

Mom peeks at the portrait in the rearview mirror and laughs, too. "It really looks just like him, Chlo."

"Thanks. I think it turned out great."

I've been thinking about what Mom said last night, about how easy it is to drift away from someone. *Too many things going on, and not enough time to do it all.* I know exactly how that feels.

"You know, Mom? I used to think that Uncle Will and his 'carpe diem' meant to cram as much as you can into a day. To shove as much excitement and energy as possible into twenty-four hours."

Mom looks at me in the rearview mirror. "You don't think that anymore?"

I shake my head. "No. I think . . . 'carpe diem' means focus on what's important. Everything else should just fall away. Like painting. Every brushstroke matters. If you try to layer on too much paint, or if you try to push the process too fast, you wind up with a mess."

Mom is quiet a moment, but she says, "Good thinking."

Okay, that's a good sign, her agreeing with me. I take a deep breath. "Mom, I want to quit soccer."

Mom blinks, and I can see her pause in the rearview mirror. "Are you sure? You used to love it."

I shrug. "I like it. But I feel like I'm doing too much. *We're* doing too much."

"Well, I agree with that," Mom mutters.

"I think . . . I want to spend more time making things. Making art." I don't add how Uncle Will called me the "fellow family artist," but it feels like we're both thinking it.

Mom smiles. It's not a full smile, not yet, but she'll get used to this. I just know it. "Okay. Finish out this season, and we'll retire your jersey. Your dad will be upset," she warns, eyeing me again in the mirror.

"I'll handle Dad," I say. And I will.

"What about Audrey? And your teammates?"

"I see them all in school. And I have art with Audrey. I won't let those friendships fade away. I promise." And I won't.

At school, Mom pulls into a parking spot rather than making me gather all my things and jump out in the car drop-off line. (Every parent knows you don't mess with the car drop-off line.) She unbuckles Uncle Will's portrait and looks at it a moment before handing it to me. She lightly touches the painting of Charlie, head cocked, perched on his shoulder.

"I know why Will left you that bird."

"Yeah?"

"You two were a team, you and Will. With him gone, you wouldn't have a teammate. I know how the pairs line up: it's always been me and Gram, and Uncle Frank and Jacob, and you and Uncle Will. He left you Charlie so you wouldn't be alone. So you'd still be part of a team."

I smile. The tears still sting, even after you know the truth. I guess that's the thing about tears: they're there to remind you that the love is still there, too. And that's okay. I want the love to still be there.

Grief sometimes looks like anger, and sometimes looks like forgiveness, and sometimes looks like love. Grief doesn't go away, it just changes shape.

Mom runs a light finger over the whole painting. "You worked on this a long time."

"Grief takes time. So does painting."

When I get to art class, Ms. Umar claps her hands as our paintings enter the room. "Lovely! Beautiful! Gorgeous! I can feel the heroism beaming off these canvases, friends. Now. Let's each take a moment to stand up here"—she gestures to the front—"and tell the class a bit about our hero. Just a sentence or two. Who wants to go first?"

Hands shoot into the air. I gulp. I'm not ready to talk about Uncle Will. Not yet! I'll cry in front of a class full of my peers. Nope. No way. I sit and listen to stories of grandparents and parents and even a couple of YouTubers. My palms sweat and my stomach churns.

More and more of my classmates are done and have hung their painting on the classroom gallery wall. Ms. Umar scans the room and—*drat*! Why did I lock eyes with her?!

"Ms. Alvarez," she says, turning her smile toward me. "Would you like to go next?"

I gulp, shrug, and lug myself toward the front of the room. As I trudge up there, I have an idea.

"May I use my phone, Ms. Umar? I promise it relates to the assignment."

Ms. Umar narrows her eyes a bit, but nods. "If it relates to the assignment, then yes, Chloe."

I prop the picture of Uncle Will on the easel and push play on a snapshot I recorded this morning with my family's help:

Our power went out in Hurricane Ian. Uncle Will made his way through flooding to get to our house. Oooh, Grammy was so mad at him! Remember, Gram?
I do, Grammy says. *He should've stayed put at his place.*

But Will grinned and said, "I brought peanut butter pie!"

And he had. He brought us peanut butter pie in a hurricane. We ate it by candlelight. We played poker. We laughed as Will told us a story of Mom and Uncle Frank dutifully doing all their chores growing up, and Uncle Will being punished by getting sent to his room.

What I didn't know was Willie LOVED his room, Grammy chimes in. *Had a whole library up there full of those paperback mysteries.* She chuckles. *He'd sit up there and read and laugh and Frank and I would be so mad,* Mom adds. *He got away with that for YEARS.*

Years, Uncle Frank agrees.

The next day, the roads were still flooded. We heard some meowing outside. A kitten was stranded on top of an air-conditioning unit on the house across the alley. Uncle Will waded out in that nasty floodwater up to his thighs, to get the kitten. That water was strong, too—he shouldn't have gone out in it. Grammy was boiling mad at him—

Yep! Grammy chimes in.

—but he brought the kitten back. "Aren't you a friendly girl?" Uncle Will asked the kitten, who crawled into the front pocket of his sweatshirt and

wouldn't come out for three hours. The kitten had no collar and, we found out later, no microchip to locate an owner.
And that's how we got my cat, Friendly.

The voice recorder stops. I thought if I didn't talk, I wouldn't cry, but I'm fighting tears anyway.

Ms. Umar clasps her hands at her chest and bounces on her toes, her jewelry clanging. "Yes! Yes! Everyday heroes! We don't give enough credit to the woman who picks up trash in the park, or the kid who invites the new student to eat lunch, or the guy who rescues the kitten. Well done, Chloe. Well done."

I blink. Too much. I pick up my painting to hang it on the wall, and when I turn, Audrey stands and slow-claps. No one else joins her, but I think it still counts? I got a standing ovation!

Uncle Frank surprises me after school. He pulls his shiny SUV up next to me in the bus line and smiles wide. "Hop in." I don't care if I get another round of After School Service for hopping out of the bus line. I do it.

He drives through the narrow streets of Charleston, and we slide up in front of Shakey's Ice Cream Parlor. The bell rings when we enter.

Uncle Frank pulls a beat-up piece of paper out of

his jacket pocket and unfolds it on the counter inside. He looks at me. "I found Will's list. Looks like he had some unfinished business. I intend to finish it. Do you want mint chocolate chip?"

I shake my head, eyes stinging. "Nah. Let's finish the list together. I'll go with bubble gum. Carpe diem!"

Uncle Frank beams. "Carpe diem!"

41

NO MORE MYSTERIES?

Our backyard crackles with laughter and energy. White lights twinkle around the edge of the patio. Smoke sizzles from the grill. Music spills out through the screen door. Mom decided we needed some fun, so we're throwing an end-of-school/beginning-of-summer party. My soccer friends Emmi, Audrey, and Lydia play cornhole with now pink-haired Kiley and Uncle Frank, while Jacob acts out (overly so) us spying on Kiley through the windows of Grounded.

"And then she threatened us with a knife!"

Emmi and Audrey gasp and look at Kiley, who laughs. "No, I didn't. I was holding a knife when you came in."

Jacob darts his eyes to my friends and back to Kiley, then shrugs. "Sure, that's your take."

Audrey whacks my arm with the back of her hand. "Chloe Alvarez. Don't you *ever* investigate a murder without me, you hear? You know I'd be a great detective. I even dressed as Sherlock Holmes for Character Day."

I laugh. "You got it."

She runs off, joining Jacob at the firepit and laughing too loudly at his impressions. Ew.

George Jones the landlord hovers (and hoovers) over the food table, and he can't stop talking about how delicious Uncle Frank's smoked chicken wings are. "In a nutshell," George Jones says, sucking sauce off his fingers, "these are the best chicken wings I ever did eat." He's always *right there* with those metaphors, but not quite? I smile. Mr. Cheatham, Uncle Will's lawyer, agrees while gnawing on a chicken bone.

Deloris the psychic reads tarot cards on our picnic table, flipping the colorful cards and huffing on a vape pen, which grosses me out. Boring Boris is totally absorbed by his reading, convinced that he has unknown enemies lurking in the shadows, spying on him. If he only knew! And Deloris does *not* look like Jabba the Hutt. She's young, like maybe twenty-five, with long dark hair and sparkling dark eyes, and she's wearing leather pants and a T-shirt that says, in big block letters, *I KNOW*.

"Ah, what's this?" Uncle Frank asks loudly. He pulls a tarot card from behind his ear with a flourish and bows as he gives it to Deloris. Everyone claps, and Uncle Frank winks at Jacob and gives him the double guns. "Counting on you to assist me in a magic show later, buddy!"

Jacob burns about sixty shades of red and shakes his head so hard, I fear it might fly off. "Nope," he says. "Nuh-uh." I laugh. Jacob's secret magical past makes every part of me smile.

Charlie rides around on Friendly's back, a new trick she's learned. Friendly is, of course, not a fan of this mode of transportation; she slinks and curls, but Charlie manages to balance like she's riding a skateboard.

"Alexa, play Pink Floyd!" she squawks. The music switches.

Number 13 Boring Boris shakes his head, his long locks swaying over his shoulders. "That dang bird."

Mom laughs. "That dang bird."

Everyone gets real still when Jaws and her beefy grandson walk in, but Grammy quickly steps forward: "Care to play some blackjack, Mildred?"

Mildred flips open the purse she clutches and produces some cards. "Brought my own deck."

I couldn't believe it when Grammy said she wanted to invite Mildred and her grandson to the party. Mildred had apparently cornered Grammy at the senior center and, while she didn't exactly apologize, said something along the lines of "I didn't know Will was your son at first, when I gave him that money. I'da told him to go to you, that you'd understand. That you'd *want* to help. The money I gave him? He never really said, but I think it was for medical bills. But he didn't want to worry y'all." Grammy insisted on inviting her after that. "I don't know how she treats others, Chloe-bug," she told me. "But she helped Will out when he thought he couldn't come to us. That means something."

So Jaws was invited, after swearing up and down to Grammy that she's stopped playing the role of loan shark. I still plan on keeping her far away from Charlie. And butter knives.

Jaws walks by the portrait of Uncle Will, perched on a side table, looking out at us all. He's now sporting a shiny blue ribbon from the all-district art fair. I couldn't believe it when Ms. Umar chose Uncle Will's portrait for the show, and I double couldn't believe it when it *won*! Jaws pauses. "Looks just like him. He was a good guy."

I shake my head and chuckle. Three weeks ago, I would've never imagined *this* group of folks at our summer kickoff party. Grief feels so awful, but it can also bring you the most unlikely friends.

My memory snapshots to Uncle Will, gently pulling aside a thorny branch, a tangle of twigs in one of Mom's knockout rosebushes that line our backyard. *Look, Chlo! There's a whole nest of babies in there! Think about what those birds have to go through every time they come and go from this nest—all those thorns! But they're safe in here. They're together.*

"What a motley crew," I mutter.

"Alexa, play Mötley Crüe!" Charlie squawks from Friendly's back. Alexa chooses "Shout at the Devil," and Grammy and Jaws belt the lyrics from the poker table.

The stories turn to why they all made the suspects list. George Jones pounds the table with the palm of his hand and shouts, "Well, I'll be crocodile's uncle! I've never been a murder suspect before."

"Me neither," Kiley laughs.

Jaws shifts the wrinkles on her face. "I have."

But then she splits apart with laughter. When Grammy laughs, I do, too. But I don't know if Jaws was serious. I suppose I don't really want to know.

We laugh, we cry, we eat chicken wings. I sigh, full and happy. Mom gathers up a round of plates and cups and heads inside.

"The only thing I don't get is the yellow Prius," I say. "Why was it following us?"

"Yeah," Jacob says. "That car was *everywhere*. Total spy stuff."

Jaws smirks, shrugs. "Wanna know who was driving?"

"YES!" Jacob, Uncle Frank, Grammy, and I all shout. I about leap out of my skin trying to move closer to this loan shark.

"Car was rented to *Teresa Calhoun Alvarez*. Sounds like an inside job to me, heh-heh."

You know those moments where everything seems to screech to a halt, like the sound of slamming brakes on a heavy car just before the crash? This is that moment.

Mom appears in the doorway. We all turn, slowly, slowly, and look at her. She blinks, chuckles. "What?"

"Mom," I say. "What kind of car are you driving?"

Mom's eyebrows knit together. "A Prius. You know that."

Jacob arches an eyebrow. "What color?"

Mom blinks. "Right now? Yellow."

Then, the crash.

Jacob throws his hands in the air. "What?!"

Uncle Frank looks dumbfounded. "You gotta be kidding me."

Grammy places her fists on her hips. "A yellow Prius? Honestly, Teresa?"

I am, for once, speechless.

Mom holds up a single finger, *one minute*. She dashes inside, fishes around in the key bowl, and comes back with her key fob. She aims it up the street and clicks.

A yellow Prius parked far up the road, one we didn't see before since we've let our suspicions down, sings *beep-beep!*

"Beep-beep!" Charlie echoes from the edge of the picnic table.

My mouth falls open. I look to Jacob, Grammy, and Uncle Frank. They're speechless, too.

Mom looks smug. "*That* yellow Prius?"

"Teresa," Uncle Frank says at last. "When did you get a new car?"

"I didn't. It's a rental."

"But . . . ," I say. But I don't know how to finish that thought, so it just hangs there. *But . . .* Finally I find the words: "Why were you following us?"

Mom is holding back the world's biggest smile, I can tell. "I thought y'all saw me. At Shorty's? I'd make a better spy than I thought!"

Jacob blinks. "You were *following* us?"

Mom shrugs sheepishly. "Oh, come on. You, taking your sister to get coffee *before school*? I knew y'all were up to something. I wanted to know what. And then you kept sneaking around together. So I kept following. I really thought you'd invite me along if you saw me." The way she says that makes my heart ping a little.

"But where's your car?" I ask. "Your white Prius?"

Mom gets flustered now. "In the shop, y'all. Seriously. I've been driving that rental for three weeks now and not a one of y'all noticed? And you thought you'd solve a *murder*?"

Ouch. But Uncle Frank laughs, then Jacob, then me. Mom shakes her head at our team of detectives. "Chloe, you're right. We are *way* too busy if none of you noticed I'm driving a different car."

Grammy shakes her head, her lips pursed. She's trying not to laugh as well. "You followed us? Sneaky! You're grounded, Teresa!" Grammy likes to threaten her forty-five-year-old daughter like that all the time.

Mom laughs. "Mother. *You rode in that car last week*. When we went to Will's apartment."

Uncle Frank, Jacob, and I all turn to Grammy. She looks at us in surprise. But she quickly rearranges her face to look annoyed and waves us off with a flick of her hand.

"Yellow . . . white . . . y'all know I'm colorblind. How am I supposed to notice something like that?"

We all look at each other, then talk over one another: "NO, we didn't know that!" "You're colorblind?!" "Mother! Geez, no."

Uncle Frank tilts his head at Mom. "Why didn't you just join us? If you knew we were up to something? You had to have seen us chasing you."

Mom shrugs. "I figured you guys would've invited me if you wanted me there. But truly, it was because of Chloe."

"Me?" I say, blinking rapidly. "It wasn't my idea to leave you out! I promise!"

Mom smiles and shakes her head. "No, I mean—it was the first time I'd seen you look happy since Will died. Well, maybe not exactly *happy*, but . . ."

I throw my arms around her and squeeze extra tight. I know what she means. "But not miserable. It was good to have something to focus on besides just missing Will. Murder is distracting."

Our guests are crying laughing at our family's antics. The five of us—Jacob, Mom, Uncle Frank, Grammy, and I—shift our gazes at each other, then burst out laughing, too.

"Ahhhh," I breathe at last between bouts of belly-cramping laughter. "No more mysteries, then, I guess."

No more mysteries. It twists my heart. This mystery brought my family together after Uncle Will died. Without a mystery to solve, will we stay close? Or will we drift back into our old pattern of *go go go*?

Charlie always seems to sense what I'm feeling. She flaps her wings, gives a little jump off the table's edge—

—and she flies! She coasts upward onto a branch of the magnolia tree in the corner of our yard. She seems surprised by this new ability, and she wobbles as she gets a foothold on the branch.

"Marry me, Linda!" Charlie shouts from about two feet overhead. "Awk! I love you, Linda! Marry me!"

The five of us eye each other.

Mom blinks. "Linda? Did she say Linda? Who's Linda?!"

"Where's Chloe?!" Charlie squawks. I barely have time to beam that she's finally learned to place *me* in her peekaboo game. She's flapping wildly, and we can't risk her going any higher. "Peekaboo. Wheeeeeere's Chloe?" Using a step stool, I climb toward Charlie in the magnolia tree.

"Here I am," I whisper. "Peekaboo. Here I am." Charlie hops on my arm and clutches my skin like it's also a tree branch. I wince. She's shaking, and her feathers ripple like sand in wind. I take her and place her gently in her cage inside. She hides in the back corner, tucks her head under her wing, and falls asleep.

Charlie's big adventure tuckered her out. But she flew! She had a taste of what that feels like, and I'm excited for her.

We'll have to trim back her flight feathers again. They've grown, just like hair or fingernails, and because of that, she was able to fly today. But she's always been a pet, so we can't let just her fly free; she'll get hurt. Though it *is* so nice to know that every once in a while, her wings will lift her higher.

It's nice to know flying is right there waiting to lift you, after just a little bit of growth.

AUTHOR'S NOTE

I took some liberties in this story for the sake of plot and pacing. I hope bird owners will forgive me for any mistakes I made regarding the care and loving maintenance of African Grey parrots. Parrots like Charlie can learn up to 1,000 words; the parrot in this story would definitely be on the higher end of the vocabulary spectrum! These are intelligent, beautiful birds; if you'd like to watch one in action, check out Einstein the Parrot's videos on YouTube: www.youtube.com/c/einsteinparrot.

Also, to the citizens of Charleston, South Carolina: I've tried my hardest to capture your beautiful city accurately. I folded several local ghostly legends into one Magnolia Cemetery ghost tour; not all of these "famous" ghosts are laid to rest in this particular graveyard. This setting was just so creepy and beautiful, I had to include it! Please also forgive any inaccuracies in directions, cross streets, parks, etc. And thanks for inventing shrimp and grits!

My apologies to the teacher of *my* teen etiquette class, Ernestine Meharry. It was actually a really fun way to pass time in the long, hot summer in a small Southern town, though my friends and I complained endlessly about those classes at the time. I've always wanted to write a story set against the backdrop of those classes; it looks like Will beat me to it!

Thank you to the friends and family who, in May 2023, sponsored me in a write-a-thon: I wrote thirty minutes a day throughout May to benefit the American Cancer Society. My gratitude goes to Cory Grisham, Emily Marek, Rhonda Roberts, and Melissa Sergio. Thank you to Shelli R. Johannes for the bird info and the decades-long friendship! Thank you to my family, always. I love you all. Family is wondrous.